A Talent for Destruction

# A Talent
# for Destruction

### Sheila Radley

*All the characters and events portrayed in this work are fictitious.*

A TALENT FOR DESTRUCTION

A Felony & Mayhem mystery

PRINTING HISTORY
First UK edition (Constable): 1982
First U.S. edition (Scribner's): 1982
Felony & Mayhem edition: 2008

ISBN: 978-1-934609-16-3

Manufactured in the United States of America

The icon above says you're holding a book in the Felony & Mayhem "British" category. These books are set in or around the UK, and feature the highly literate, often witty prose that fans of British mystery demand. Other "British" titles from F&M include:

**MICHAEL DAVID ANTHONY**
*The Becket Factor*

**ROBERT BARNARD**
*Death on the High C's*
*Out of the Blackout*
*Death and the Chaste Apprentice*
*The Skeleton in the Grass*
*Corpse in a Gilded Cage*

**LIZA CODY**
*Dupe*

**PETER DICKINSON**
*King and Joker*
*The Old English Peep Show*
*Skin Deep*

**CAROLINE GRAHAM**
*The Killings at Badger's Drift*
*Death of a Hollow Man*
*Murder at Madingley Grange*
*Death in Disguise*
*Written in Blood*

**REGINALD HILL**
*Death of a Dormouse*
*A Clubbable Woman*
*An Advancement of Learning*
*Ruling Passion*

**ELIZABETH IRONSIDE**
*Death in the Garden*
*The Accomplice*
*A Very Private Enterprise*

**JOHN MALCOLM**
*A Back Room in Somers Town*

**JANET NEEL**
*Death's Bright Angel*

**SHEILA RADLEY**
*Death in the Morning*
*The Chief Inspector's Daughter*

For more information, please visit us online at
www.FelonyAndMayhem.com

Or write to us at:

Felony and Mayhem Press
156 Waverly Place • New York, NY 10014

# A Talent for Destruction

A minister shall not give himself to such occupations, habits, or recreations as do not befit his sacred calling, or may be detrimental to the performance of the duties of his office, or tend to be a just cause of offence to others; and at all times he shall be diligent to frame and fashion his life and that of his family according to the doctrine of Christ, and to make himself and them, as much as in him lies, wholesome examples and patterns to the flock of Christ.

Canon Law of the Church of England, C.26.2

# Part 1—This Winter

# Chapter 1

The children had never seen so much snow.

It began just in time for the start of the Christmas holidays, falling so lightly at first that it did no more than tickle their upturned faces as they ran out of school, tantalizing them with the possibility of a different world of play: snowballing in the streets, building snowmen in the gardens, tobogganing in Castle Meadow, even sliding on the ice if the Mere froze over. But although the darkening sky looked full of it, and the air tasted cold and thick and still, the first fall of snow was hesitant. From the gates of the primary school, built in the expansive 1960s on the outskirts of Breckham Market, the children looked out across ploughed fields and saw with disappointment that the snow had done no more than dust the dark earth, like caster sugar sprinkled on Christmas pudding.

But that evening the wind rose, the snow beat down in a blizzard, and next morning the town—the whole of East Anglia—woke to pale empty skies and silence. Roads and paths and gardens were obliterated, houses were huddled under thick white thatch, every telegraph and electricity line supported a narrow wall of snow. Cars that had been left outside overnight were transformed into mobile igloos. In the centre of the small town the parish church of St Botolph, standing high on the top of Market

Hill, pinnacled and battlemented and soaringly Perpendicular, had been softened and rounded into lines that made it seem almost Baroque.

The children were overjoyed. They bounced outside, wellington-booted and plumped up with extra woollens and scarves, to do battle, or more peaceably to roll giant snowballs. Down by the slow black river, Castle Meadow—the site of a minor twelfth-century fortification whose grassed-over ruins no archaeologist had ever found time to excavate—provided useful slopes for toboggans improvised from melamine trays and plastic fertilizer sacks. Some children hastily amended their Christmas present lists to include proper toboggans. All of them crossed their fingers in the hope that the snow would stay at least until the end of the holidays.

And the snow did stay, for weeks, bonded to the surfaces where it had fallen by exceptionally severe frosts. Ice covered the surface of the Mere to a depth of several inches, and made roads and paths hazardous. It was the hardest winter for eighteen years, a particularly difficult time for the old and infirm, for those who had to travel to work, and for farmers with livestock out in the fields.

It was a cruel winter for wild creatures, too. Emboldened by hunger, everything that flew or ran or crawled began to draw near human habitation. Mallard ducks, dispossessed from the Mere by the ice, besieged the executive houses on Mere Road. Small birds braved cats in order to snatch crumbs thrown from back doors. Backyard hens were nudged from their feeding troughs by families of rats. A fox was seen in broad daylight, scavenging round the dustbins at the back of the golf club. Only the carrion crows lived well, gorging themselves on the carcasses of whatever succumbed to hunger and cold.

But for the children, the weather remained a delight. The start of the school term was an unwelcome intrusion upon their activities, because it seemed impossible that the freeze could last until the half-term holiday. Those who had managed to acquire proper toboggans felt a particular sense of frustration as they looked out of their classroom windows and saw all that snow going to waste.

One of the chief mourners was Justin Muttock, aged ten. His grandfather, a carpenter by trade, had made him a toboggan for Christmas, and he had shared the rides with his friend Adrian Orris. Adrian was a little older and a little taller, the leader in all their ploys until now, and so Justin had a double reason for wanting the snow to remain: the unaccustomed power of patronage, generously bestowed or capriciously withheld, was as sweet to him as the swish of snow under the runners and the rush of cold air against his face.

To his disappointment, a slow thaw began in mid-February. The sky lightened; the sun offered to shine. Trees became black rather than white, and the deceptively soft-looking paws of snow that had for weeks pressed down the branches of garden conifers, threatening to break them, gave up and slid limply off. Walls and roofs began to emerge, like buildings partially excavated from a bed of white lava. Justin's front-garden snowman still retained its hard-packed dignity, but the white carpet it had stood on was beginning to look threadbare. Patches of deep snow lingered in places, but Castle Meadow was on a south-facing slope and the boys' hopes receded with the strengthening of the sun. Most of the other open spaces in or near the town were too flat for tobogganing.

And then, on the first day of the half-term holiday, he remembered Parson's Close.

'Bet there's still enough snow there!' he told Adrian.

'There's a good slope, and big old trees at the top so the sun can't shine through.'

'We can't go to Parson's Close,' said his friend. 'You know what that man said he'd do if he caught us there again.'

'That was last summer—he won't be there in this weather, stupid! Anyway, we only want to use the toboggan. We can't get wrong for doing that.'

'We might if the Rector sees us,' objected Adrian. It was not a possibility that really worried him, but Justin's idea was a good one and because it was not his own he wanted to diminish it.

But six weeks of uncontested leadership had heightened Justin's estimation of himself by several inches. 'He won't see us, not from his house. I'm going anyway, even if you're not.'

Anonymous in their dark green parkas, the boys hurried through the streets one behind the other, carrying the toboggan so as not to scrape its runners on the bare patches of pavement that had begun to appear through the gritty slush. The sky was a cool clear blue, and the town smelled of wet wood. Melting snow dripped on to pedestrians from the timber-framed overhangs of the old shops in the Shambles, and trickled down the gutters of Market Hill.

The boys stopped for a breather under the great tower of the church, then shifted their grip and set off again, leaving the shopping streets and turning right past a no-through-road sign on to less well-trodden, whiter slush; along the quietness of St Botolph Street, beside the flint wall that bordered first the churchyard, then the extensive gardens of the Rectory. On the opposite side of the road was a survival oddly rural so near the centre of the town: a high chestnut-paling fence, overhung by bare-branched trees. In the middle of the fencing was a five-barred gate, with a meadow beyond. The painted word PRIVATE on the top bar was faded, but still clearly visible.

The boys ignored the gate, and continued along the cul-de-sac. Across the end of it was a hedge, with a gap in the middle opening on to a footpath that sloped down through some allotment gardens. As they drew level with the place where the roadway ended and the fence formed a right angle with the hedge, the boys took a swift glance round to make sure that they were not being watched, tugged two loose palings aside and pushed their way through the fence into Parson's Close.

As Justin had predicted, here was untrodden snow. The meadow faced north, sloping down from St Botolph Street towards the by-pass, and the snow was best at the top, where a row of mature copper beech trees cut off most of the sun. At the bottom of the meadow, where bramble bushes sprawled beside the ditch that separated Parson's Close from the grass verge of the by-pass, the snow had almost gone; but there was still enough of it to make a longer toboggan run than Castle Meadow had ever offered.

It proved to be hard work. The snow was powdery stuff, crusted on top, and at first the toboggan simply sank in. But the boys persevered, and by the end of the morning their solo runs had almost reached the bottom of the meadow.

Their last ride before they went home in search of dinner was made together. Justin sat in front. Adrian gave him a running push and jumped on behind. The extra weight added to their momentum and they slid nearly the full length of the meadow, bumping and jolting and cheering until the toboggan finally hit a tussock of grass and overturned, tumbling them out almost in the bushes.

They lay for some minutes where they had fallen, sprawled on a thin cushion of snow, gasping and laughing and throwing weak punches at each other, and kicking their legs in the air.

'Cor, I'm hot,' said Justin, sitting up red-cheeked and pushing back the fur-lined hood of his parka. Then, 'Blast, now I'm caught on a bramble.'

A long woody shoot, trailing out from the nearest bush, was hooked by its thorns to his hood. He turned and pulled himself free, and as he did so he noticed something round and yellowish-white lying beside a heap of rubbish under the bare purple branches of the bush.

'Hey, there's a football!' he said excitedly. 'Somebody must have lost it.'

Adrian got up to look. 'That it's not,' he said, reasserting his authority. 'How can it be? It's not round all over—and anyway, it's got a hole in it.'

'What is it, then?'

'I dunno. My legs are longer than yours, I'll see if I can get it out.'

Adrian reached one wellingtonned foot under the bush and hooked the object towards him. It was caught up in withered, snow-matted grass, and for a few moments it resisted. Then it rolled over, into full view.

The blood disappeared from Adrian's cheeks, leaving him almost as bleached as the thing that was staring sightlessly up at him. He made a small mewling sound and took several steps backwards. Then he turned and fled up the hill, floundering through the snow, yammering with fright.

In a second Justin was after him, sobbing and stumbling and screaming, 'Wait for me!' His toboggan lay forgotten in the last of the snow. He, too, had peered into the bush and had seen the eyeless, noseless sockets, the grinning teeth below the rounded cranium.

# Chapter 2

Detective Chief Inspector Douglas Quantrill was on the carpet. Specifically, he was on the doorstep of the grey-brick, early Victorian Rectory, having been summoned by the Rector to discuss several hundred pounds' worth of damage to the church hall, apparently sustained when the youth club got out of hand the previous evening. It was not a matter with which the head of Breckham Market CID would normally deal in person; he was there because the Rector suspected that one of the ringleaders was the Chief Inspector's son Peter.

The door was opened by the Rector's wife, Gillian Ainger. Quantrill was not a churchgoer, nor on social terms with the Aingers, but it was a small town and he knew her by sight, as she knew him.

'Ah, Mr Quantrill—do please come in. I'm afraid my husband has been called away unexpectedly. He asked me to apologize if he wasn't back in time, but I'm sure he won't be long. A man from Furze Close was rushed into hospital at Yarchester last night with a heart attack, and his wife went with him in the ambulance. His condition has stabilized, fortunately, but his wife was stuck at the hospital so she rang Robin and asked him to fetch her.'

'One of your husband's congregation?' Quantrill asked, wiping his shoes on the outsize doormat and hanging his overcoat where she indicated, on a row of hooks long enough to accommodate the coats of the entire parochial church council.

'No. But no one else's either. The whole town's our parish, and in times of crisis people do tend to remember that they're nominally Church of England.'

'A parson must have a lot of demands made on him,' commented Quantrill, offering heavily polite conversation rather than sympathy. He felt uneasy, anxious to get on with the interview.

One corner of her mouth lifted in a very strained smile. 'Yes, he does.'

She was about thirty-five or -six, at least ten years younger than Quantrill. Her figure was sturdy, and she obviously took no interest in clothes. Her fair hair was tied back loosely at the nape of her neck in a style that suits a mature woman only if she has a particularly good bone structure, and Gillian Ainger had not. She gave the impression of having chosen her hair-style and her pale lipstick at the age of eighteen, and of having thought no more about them. And yet she had a pleasant open face, with smallish but widely spaced hazel eyes and a generous mouth. If she bothered, Quantrill thought, she could look attractive.

But perhaps her husband gave her no encouragement. As he himself had discovered—belatedly, after twenty-odd years of marriage—it seems to make a disproportionate amount of difference to a woman if her husband takes a bit of notice of her. For a start, it might make Mrs Ainger look happier. The lines at each side of her mouth were deeper than her age warranted, and she looked dark and tired round the eyes.

She had led him down the wide chilly hall, floored with Victorian encaustic tiles, and into a sparsely furnished

study. 'Can I get you a cup of coffee while you're waiting?' she asked, as she lit the gas fire.

'Thank you, but I've just had one.' The Chief
Inspector had already called at the church hall and seen
the damage that had been done there. The allegation
against Peter was serious, and he didn't want either of the
Aingers to think that he was treating the interview as a
social occasion. And presumably Gillian Ainger knew
about the trouble at the youth club. From all that he'd
ever heard in the town, she played the conventional, sup-
portive role of the parson's wife. She was part of the
team, sharing the social-work aspect of the job with her
husband and knowing as much if not more about the
parish than he did.

The telephone rang. Quantrill stood with his back to
her while she answered it, looking out of the window at
an expanse of virgin snow that was shrinking round the
edges, but still covered most of the garden. The only footprints on it were those of birds and small animals,
because the Aingers had no children. A shame to see all
that unused snow, he thought; there had never been
enough of it when he was a boy. Not that the appeal of
snow lasted very long for youngsters. It was a thousand
pities that young Peter wasn't still content with the harm-
less pleasures of snowfights and tobogganing, instead of
getting his kicks from helping to break up the church hall.
*Allegedly* helping to break up the church hall.

Behind him, Mrs Ainger was dealing competently and
patiently with some kind of parish problem: listening,
soothing, advising, co-operating. An ideal wife for a busy
parson—she could probably take the services just as well
as her husband, too, if anyone gave her a chance,
Quantrill thought. Having been brought up in a
Nonconformist family he was not even nominally C of E,

and so he could afford to take a liberal view on the ordination of women.

From the hall outside, there came a sudden irascible shout and a clattering noise. Mrs Ainger stopped in mid-sentence, the telephone receiver in her hand, and glanced with exasperation at the door. There was another cry, and this time it sounded like pain. Quantrill gave her an interrogative glance, but, without waiting for her reaction, took it upon himself to open the door and find out what was happening.

A big-boned, scrawny old man sat at the turn of the wide staircase, fully dressed except that one foot was bare and the other was half in, half out of, a sock. One slipper, fallen or flung, lay on the hall floor, the other on the second step. He was rocking and wailing, nursing his bare mottled foot in both hands.

'Are you all right?' asked Quantrill, taking the stairs two at a time and putting one hand on his shoulder. The old man squinted up at him through ferociously tufted eyebrows, and immediately quietened. The slack folds of his face were unshaven, and he smelled of tobacco and, faintly, of urine.

'She's hidden me shoes,' he said in a hoarse whisper. 'I want me shoes, and she won't let me have 'em. I want to go *out*.'

There was a ping as Mrs Ainger put down the telephone and came into the hall. Immediately, he resumed his noisy performance: 'Oh, oh, oh, I've hurt me foot. I can't find me shoes and me slippers are loose, and now I've fallen down the stairs and hurt me foot. Oh, it hurts.' He spied down at her, assessing the effect he was having, and Quantrill retreated to ground level, out of the way.

'Stop making such a fuss, Dad,' she said evenly. 'The

pavements are still far too slippery. It's not safe for you to
go out on your own.'

'I haven't been out for months and months,' he grumbled childishly. 'Not for months.'

'It's been snowing since before Christmas,' she pointed out.

'Not for months before that, either. Not since last
summer...'

'But that,' she reminded him, 'was because you'd hurt
your back. And anyway, you're exaggerating. One or
other of us has taken you out in the car at least once a
week—'

'That don't count. I don't want to be taken out by *him*
and made to sit in a posh pub with a bloody *carpet* on the
floor, and I don't want to drink the fizzy muck he thinks
is beer. I want to walk as far as the Boot and meet folks
as'll talk to me, and drink pints o' draught bitter and—
and spit on the floor if I feel like it!'

The old man's face had coloured with genuine passion
and now, suddenly and deliberately, he spat on the tiles of
the hall. His daughter froze. She was white except for a
splotch of angry colour on either cheek. Quantrill stood
still, trying—as far as it was possible for a man of his
height and weight—to pretend that he wasn't there. Only
his eyes moved, from father to daughter to the yellow gob
that lay on the floor between them, at once a reproach, an
insult, and a token of impotent defiance.

But the old man's rebellion collapsed as quickly as it
had begun. He started to cry, almost silently, the tears ooz-
ing down the vertical creases of his face and mingling with
residual dribble on his emery-paper chin. His daughter let
out a long breath, bent to pick up his slippers, and carried
them to where he sat hunched on the stairs, his big knot-
ted workman's hands hanging limp between his knees.

'It's all right, Dad,' she said wearily. 'Don't upset yourself. Here, put your slippers on.'

His lower lip trembled. 'I've lost me other sock.'

She retrieved it from where it had fallen, knelt down and eased his socks and slippers on to his stiff, shiny, purple feet. He wiped the cuff of his cardigan across his wet eyes.

'Will you cut me toenails tonight, dear?' he supplicated.

Her hands were still shaking with tension, but she forced herself to smile. 'That's a farrier's job, with nails as tough as yours! You've got an appointment with the chiropodist next week, so you won't have long to wait.'

'I might make holes in me socks afore then. I don't want to give you extra work. I don't want to be a burden.'

'Don't worry about that. You go upstairs and get shaved, and then I'll make your coffee.'

'With hot milk?'

'With hot milk.'

'You're a good daughter to me, our Gilly.'

She said nothing, but watched him climb stiffly to his feet and shamble up the stairs, a great ruin of a man, his trousers slack round his bony haunches, his cardigan unevenly buttoned. Then she ran, set-faced, to the cloakroom that led off the hall, returned with a wad of toilet paper and a bottle of disinfectant, wiped the spittle off the floor, flushed the paper down the lavatory and scrubbed her hands. Only then did she acknowledge that Quantrill was still there.

'Sorry about that,' she said jerkily, without looking at him. 'It seemed inappropriate to attempt an introduction, but that was my father, Henry Bowers. He's been living with us for the past year, ever since my mother died.' One corner of her mouth gave a wry twist: 'Living and partly living... I hope you weren't too shocked.'

He shook his head reassuringly. 'Policemen don't shock so easily.'

'Oh—' Gillian Ainger coloured, suddenly confused. 'I'd quite forgotten, for a moment, what your job is.'

'I hadn't. And it's very embarrassing, I can tell you, to know that your husband suspects my son of vandalism.'

She relaxed a little, grateful that he had changed the subject; and then the front door opened and the Rector hurried in, apologizing for being late.

The Reverend Robin Ainger was a very good-looking man, nearing forty but still slim, narrow-shouldered but almost as tall as Quantrill. There was, however, something dated about his looks. His particular style of handsomeness—regular features, perfect teeth and short, cleanly parted, evenly wavy light brown hair—was one that had gone out of fashion with baggy trousers, big band sounds and cries of 'Anyone for tennis?' The outdated impression was reinforced by his tweed jacket and roll-necked sweater. Even so, it was easy to see why St Botolph's church always attracted such a loyal female congregation. The colour of the Rector's sweater exactly matched, and emphasized, the unusually pale blue of his eyes.

He greeted Quantrill with wary affability; presumably he wasn't looking forward to the interview either. Then he turned to his wife, putting a hand lightly on her shoulder. 'Everything all right, Gillian?'

She hesitated, as though wondering whether to tell him. 'Henry had a tantrum, I'm afraid—in front of Mr Quantrill.'

Her husband's hand tightened. 'He would... What about, this time?'

'Oh, the usual. Wanting to go out to the pub on his own.'

Robin Ainger looked at Quantrill defensively. 'I expect you think we're being over-protective—' he began, but Quantrill interrupted him.

'If you really want to know what I was thinking,' he said bluntly, 'it was "Thank God my poor old father didn't live that long". He died of a heart attack when he was playing bowls, at the age of sixty-eight. It was a shock for us at the time, and we grieved that he'd died so soon after retirement, but looking back I'm glad he went like that. I wouldn't wish the humiliations of old age on him, and I wouldn't want my wife to have the burden of looking after the old boy. Our Peter is quite demanding enough.'

The Rector nodded, and released Gillian's shoulder. 'Yes, I know you're a busy man, Mr Quantrill, and I'm grateful to you for calling.' He gestured the Chief Inspector into his study. 'Thank you for holding the fort,' he said to his wife. 'I think we'd all appreciate some coffee, wouldn't we? And if you wouldn't mind intercepting any calls for the next twenty minutes or so—?'

Quantrill caught a glimpse of her face as her husband closed the door: tense, anxiety-ridden, near to breaking point. In that particular partnership, he thought, it looked as though Gillian Ainger was the one on whom the greatest demands were made.

The interview was, on both sides, uncomfortable. They began with unnatural heartiness, agreeing that the church hall incident would never have occurred if the volunteer supervisor hadn't suddenly gone down with 'flu. The Rector emphasized that he had as yet no firm evidence for his suspicion that Peter Quantrill was involved, and the Chief Inspector asserted that there would be no question of whitewashing the crime just because his son might have taken part. They further agreed, over watery coffee brought in almost immediately by Mrs Ainger, that Peter was one of the liveliest of the youth-club members, and currently anti-authority.

There were, of course, mitigating circumstances. No doubt all the boys felt frustrated after weeks of being cooped up because of the bad weather; and Peter's age, fifteen, was a particularly difficult one. And then, being a policeman's son was in itself a kind of challenge. As Robin Ainger put it sociologically, adolescents always seek the approbation of the peer group. As Douglas Quantrill put it bluntly, a copper's son always feels that he has to prove himself to his mates.

'The boy was limping a bit when he came home last night, but he said nothing at all either then or this morning, so I'm grateful to you for getting in touch with me personally,' said Quantrill. 'It would have been very embarrassing if the first I knew about the damage was when I saw his name in a report from one of my men.'

'That's what I thought, otherwise I wouldn't have troubled you.' Robin Ainger flexed an ivory paperknife in his long thin fingers. 'I'm very angry about this incident, Mr Quantrill,' he went on, 'very angry indeed. The youngsters themselves have put so much time and effort into the improvement and redecoration of the church hall over the years, and I find it intolerable that an anti-social minority should—'

The Chief Inspector, for once on the wrong side of the desk, heard him out patiently with an expression that combined surrogate penitence with a reservation on his son's behalf of the right to plead Not Guilty. Listening to the Rector's tone of voice rather than to his words, he was puzzled that the two should be so much at odds. The impression that Quantrill had gained, in the four years in which Ainger had been at St Botolph's, was of a vigorous, positive, outgoing man. Now, although the Rector was voicing angry sentiments, he appeared to be completely detached from what he was saying, like an incompetent amateur actor. His eyes seemed dead behind the blue. He neither looked nor sounded angry, but as though he no longer cared.

But there were, without doubt, thought Quantrill, domestic reasons for the change in the man. Having his father-in-law living with them would be more than enough to try the charity of a saint.

'And I take it very seriously too, Mr Ainger,' the Chief Inspector concurred. 'There will be a full investigation, of course, and I shan't do it myself. I'll report the incident to my Superintendent at Yarchester, and leave him to appoint the investigating officer.'

Ainger nodded, apparently satisfied that he had made his point. 'I'd be glad if Detective Sergeant Tait did the investigation. He gave a talk to the youth club on CID work a few months ago, and the members liked him. I'm anxious not to alienate them. There's so little for them to do in the town, and if they stay away from the club because of the investigation it will have done more harm than good.'

'That's a risk we'll have to accept, I'm afraid. I've no idea who'll investigate, but it won't be Martin Tait—he's been promoted to Inspector, put back into uniform and moved to Yarchester. I can assure you that the enquiry will be done sensitively, though—we all agree with you about the value of the youth club.'

Quantrill rose to go. During the course of their conversation there had been one ring at the front door and two telephone calls, all dealt with by Mrs Ainger. Now the men heard the doorbell again, accompanied by a frenzied knocking. There were shrill voices in the hall, a moment of silence, and then the slap of running feet on the tiles.

Gillian Ainger burst into the room, her face pale, her eyes wide. She addressed her husband. 'Some boys—they say they've been playing in our meadow—they think they've found a body!'

Robin Ainger's handsome lower jaw dropped open. He focused his eyes with difficulty on his wife. He made a stammering noise, but Gillian held up her hand as if to press it against his mouth and prevent him from speaking. She shook her head vigorously, and made an effort to be calm and accurate. 'No, not a body. But it sounds as though they've found a human skull.'

Robin Ainger shut his eyes tight and swallowed hard. Quantrill strode to the door.

'Same thing, Mrs Ainger, as far as the police are concerned. Just as well I was here, it'll save you the trouble of ringing the station.'

He disappeared into the hall to talk to the boys who had brought the news, leaving the Aingers staring at each other in horrified, guilty silence.

# Chapter 3

'Rats,' said Chief Inspector Quantrill. 'Rats and carrion crows—it's been a hard winter.'

'Oh, but surely—?'

Robin Ainger was standing with him in the snow at the bottom of Parson's Close, staring at what lay under the bushes. The two boys, Justin and Adrian, having pointed out the spot from the top of the meadow, were being cared for by Mrs Ainger until a police car came to take them home. Quantrill, an investigating officer rather than a scene-of-crime specialist, was careful to disturb nothing while he waited for the arrival of his colleagues, but meanwhile he was making a few observations of his own.

'I mean—' Ainger had followed Quantrill dressed as he had been indoors, and his teeth were chattering with cold. The Chief Inspector, who was used to standing about in all weathers, had not only put on his overcoat and hat, but also changed his shoes for the wellingtons that he kept in the boot of his car. He would have thought that the Rector had conducted graveside services in winter sufficiently often to know enough to keep his feet dry; but perhaps it wasn't done for a parson to wear welly boots under his cassock.

Ainger made an effort to stop shivering, although his

face was greenish-white with chill and nausea. 'I don't know how you can be so sure that it's a comparatively recent death,' he said. 'The skeleton could be years old—half a century or more.'

Quantrill crouched down to point out what he had observed. 'No. If it had been here for any length of time, the brambles would have grown through the skull. And anyway, there's quite a lot of clothing left, and jeans with copper rivets don't date back very far. Forensic will tell us for sure, but I know that it's perfectly possible for a corpse to be reduce to a skeleton, out of doors, within a matter of weeks, let alone months. I was brought up on my father's gruesome stories of life in the trenches in the First World War, and I've had a horror of rats ever since.'

He stood up, rubbing the small of his back which had stiffened in the cold. 'A man, almost certainly, from the size of the skull; and young, I should guess, from the jeans. Well, man or woman, we've no Breckham Market people unaccounted for at present. Have we, Rector?'

The formal address helped Ainger pull himself together. 'No, not to my knowledge. If it's as recent as you think, it can't be anyone local.'

He looked round. Just beyond the bushes was a barbed-wire fence, then the snowed-over grass verge of the by-pass, built in the 1960s when the Suffolk town became an overspill area for industries and people from the crowded inner districts of north-east London. The medieval centre of the town was too narrow to take the increased volume of traffic, and the by-pass had the effect of separating the old Breckham Market from the new. 'The body could have come from anywhere,' Ainger pointed out. 'It could have been brought here by road and dumped over the barbed wire.'

Quantrill nodded. 'That sort of thing does happen—

although when a body's dumped it's usually in woodland, where there's less chance of its being found. Well, wherever it's from, this one has landed on our doorstep so we'll have to do the investigating.'

Two police cars and a van pulled up on the verge, and half a dozen policemen encumbered with equipment climbed gingerly over the barbed wire. Quantrill gave them brief instructions and they went about their work in the snow, roping off the area and setting up screens and taking photographs.

'It could have been a natural death, of course,' said Quantrill to Ainger. 'There's still the odd vagrant about who sleeps rough in the summer. One of them might have fallen ill and died here.'

'Is it possible to tell the cause of death, if the body's been reduced to a skeleton?' Ainger asked.

'It all depends—' Quantrill paused, watching for a moment as the photographer adjusted his lens for a close-up '—on what Inspector Colman and his team discover when they move the remains and search the area. There may be a meths bottle, or a hypodermic syringe, or a shotgun. And if there isn't, the pathologist may find a fracture on the skull or on the vertebrae of the neck, or a knife-nick on the ribs, that will indicate foul play. Or the chemist may find traces of poison when he analyses the soil from beneath the body. But if nothing significant is found, and there's no forensic evidence, then even the experts won't be able to tell us the cause of death.'

'There's not a lot that you personally can do, then?' Ainger asked. His teeth were chattering again, and he turned up the collar of his jacket against his wind-reddened ears and rubbed his hands together.

'Oh, there's plenty. For a start, it's my job to find out who the man was. Look, Mr Ainger, why don't you go home? I'll have to come and ask you some questions after I've seen Inspector Colman.'

'Questions?'

'Yes. This is your land, after all, so I'll have to start with you.'

'Ah, of course. Naturally, I'll do whatever I can to help. I have to go to a meeting this afternoon, but I'll be at home until about one-thirty.' Ainger noticed the toboggan that lay abandoned near the bushes. 'I may as well take this out of your way—I don't imagine the boys will want to fetch it after the fright they've had. I'll see you later, then, Mr Quantrill.'

He nodded to the Chief Inspector, took a last glance at the remains of the body, and waded up the slope towards the Rectory, tugging the toboggan behind him. On the by-pass, an unmarked car pulled in behind the police van in a spray of slush. Quantrill, his boots creaking on the snow, went to hold down the barbed wire so that his colleague Inspector Colman could climb over and join him at the start of their investigation.

Gillian Ainger was in the kitchen, going through the motions of ironing her way through a pile of her father's thick vests and long johns, but with all her senses expectant of her husband's return. As soon as she heard him open the front door she ran into the hall and silently beckoned to him to join her, hoping not to attract her father's attention.

Robin Ainger followed her into the kitchen, closed the door and leaned against it, sick and hollow-eyed.

She switched off the iron, but stood gripping it. 'Is—is it Athol?'

'I don't know. How could I tell? All I could see was a skull and what looked like a heap of old clothes.'

'What did Mr Quantrill say?'

'He was alarmingly accurate. A comparatively recent death, he decided, and a young man's. We agreed it couldn't be anyone local—'

'Did you point out that the body could have been dumped from the by-pass?'

'Yes, yes. But he thinks that's unlikely. He said that it might have been a natural death, and that even the experts may not be able to tell how death occurred. But in the meantime, he's going to ferret round and find out whose body it is... Oh God, Gillian, it'll all come out—'

He went to her and put his arms round her, but his grip was loose, almost lifeless. She rested her forehead against his shoulder for a minute and then looked up, close to tears: 'Oh, if only—'

The kitchen door opened, and Henry Bowers shuffled in. 'Is it time for me dinner yet?' he asked hopefully.

'No!' She twisted from her husband's slack arms. 'For heaven's sake, Dad, we're trying to have a private conversation. Go away! Your dinner won't be ready for half an hour.'

'But it's half-past twelve already. I'm hungry.'

'Oh—for goodness' sake—' She ran to the pantry and returned red-cheeked with tension, carrying a wire rack of newly baked cherry buns which she thrust into his hands. The old man stared down at what he held, bemused.

'Is this me dinner?'

'Yes, if you can't wait. They're your favourites, aren't they? You're always asking me to make them.'

His tongue licked slowly across his dark lips as the warm smell of the golden-brown cakes, each one topped with half a glacé cherry, brought saliva into his mouth. 'How many can I have?'

'The lot, for all I care. You're the only one I make them for. Go on, take them away.'

He looked at her, half gleeful, half puzzled. 'I shall have to have a drink. I can't eat 'em without.'

'I'll *bring* you a drink. I'll put the kettle on and make a pot of tea and bring it up to your room...if only you'll *go*.'

Her father shook his head. 'Rum sort o' dinner,' he reflected aloud. 'Bloody rum sort o' dinner, if you ask me.' But he went, almost with alacrity, as if he was afraid she might change her mind.

As the door closed she stumbled to her husband, blind with tears, and this time he held her as though he meant it. 'Don't, my love,' he muttered against her hair. 'Don't cry—you've been so brave.'

She raised her face, plainer than usual because it was blotched with emotion. 'Do you love me, Robin?'

His hands slackened. 'You know I do.'

'Then say it,' she begged. 'Say you love me.'

Robin Ainger drew a deep, shuddering breath, and expelled it in a sigh. 'I love you, and I need you. We need each other, because the Chief Inspector will be coming back at lunchtime to talk about the body.'

Her hand flew up to her mouth as though she intended to bite off all her nails at once in an access of anxiety. 'Why? Why is he coming straight here?'

'Only because the body was found in the Close. He doesn't suspect anything, he's just making routine enquiries. But we must get our story straight.' He shuddered again. 'What are we going to say? What on earth are we going to say?'

She stood back, calmer now, having taken strength from his uncertainty.

'We must say as little as possible. And to begin with, we must deny any knowledge of the body. After all, how do we know *whose* skeleton they've found? They probably won't be able to identify it—Athol wasn't English and he had no friends in Breckham. We'll be all right if we keep our heads.'

'Yes...that's it.' He reached out his hand and stroked her hair. 'We'll be all right as long as we stick together. We've proved that, haven't we? We've been through hell together, but we've come out the other side and nothing's going to break us up now. Is it?'

The Aingers stood clasped together for a few moments, Gillian's anguished eyes looking in one direction, Robin's handsome face staring bleakly in another. And then the door opened.

'Is the kettle boiling yet? I want me cup o' tea.'

# Chapter 4

The over-spiced smell of canned oxtail soup drifted down the hall as Gillian Ainger opened the front door to Chief Inspector Quantrill. She greeted him almost gaily: 'Hallo again. Come in, you're just in time to join us for lunch.'

Quantrill, exuding cold air, protested politely but was glad to take off his outdoor clothes and follow her into the kitchen. It was a large square room, more comfortable than efficient. Robin Ainger stood by the Aga, upright and handsome in dark grey suit and clerical collar, stirring the contents of a saucepan. 'Just in time,' he said, his voice as bright as his wife's. 'It's only a scratch meal, because we both have meetings to go to, but you're welcome to share it.'

'Very kind of you.' Quantrill rubbed some warmth into his hands and watched Gillian Ainger as she moved about the kitchen, putting wholemeal bread and cheese and fruit on the table. She had exchanged her old tweed skirt and sweater for a woollen dress, and had applied more lipstick. Her cheeks were warm, her eyes shining. But her brightness was obviously forced; her eyelids were swollen with crying.

She caught his glance, and smiled brilliantly. 'Robin and I were saying, just before you arrived, that we feel almost as though we're on holiday. This is the first time since Dad's been living with us that we've had lunch without him. He loves his food, but he couldn't wait for it today and he stuffed himself so full of cake half an hour ago that he's asleep now.'

Her husband brought the soup to the table in pottery mugs. 'He'll be livid when he wakes up and finds that he's missed a meal and we're both out.'

'It won't hurt him to forage for himself for once—he's not helpless yet, thank goodness, though he sometimes likes to give that impression. Let's make the most of having a meal without him.'

'I'm sorry to have interrupted this occasion, then,' said Quantrill. 'You must have little enough time to yourselves.'

The Aingers' eyes met for a second, and then they both dismissed his apology. 'It's not that we're wanting to be on our own,' Robin assured him, laughing. 'Good heavens, we've been married for sixteen years. It's just that poor old Henry's conversation gets us down, doesn't it, dear? Well, yes, that's an understatement...as you say, let's make the most of his absence. Now, Mr Quantrill, cheddar—or would you like to tackle some very ripe Camembert? This was a gift from one of my parishioners—'

For the next few minutes the conversation was social, with Ainger dominating it. He had a strong, musical voice, and was obviously accustomed to a captive audience. Quantrill guessed that he was working on the reassumption of some of the status he had lost when he stood sick and shivering in the snow, looking at the human remains.

Quantrill himself felt unusually cheerful. The sight of a corpse always made him sombre. The bodies he usually saw in the course of his work, however grotesque in their attitude of death, were recognizable as human beings: people whose lives had ended abruptly within the last few hours or days, people who had local families and friends to grieve over them. In those circumstances, cheerfulness was inappropriate.

A skeleton, though, was different. The remains that Inspector Colman's men had carefully lifted from under the bush at the bottom of Parson's Close had once been some mother's son; probably some woman's lover, some child's father. No doubt someone, somewhere, was bereft. But it was all at a distance. For once, Quantrill would not have the harrowing job of breaking the bad news. For once this was nothing more than an interesting case of unexplained death, and he could pursue his investigation without considering anyone's feelings.

He made the point to Robin Ainger. 'And you must be glad,' he added, 'that it isn't one of your parishioners.'

Before Ainger could reply the doorbell rang. He went to answer it while his wife made coffee.

'That was the local newspaper reporter,' he said when he returned. His eyes were dull again.

'What did you tell him?' his wife demanded.

'That Chief Inspector Quantrill was having lunch with us, and that no doubt he'd be making a statement in due course. There's nothing else I *could* say—I didn't want to name the boys who found the body, they're badly upset.'

Quantrill looked up. 'Have you talked to them?'

'Yes, when I returned their toboggan. They both go to our Sunday school, off and on, and I wanted to make sure they were all right. I know that both their mothers go out to work, but they were with Justin's grandmother so they'll be well looked after. I wondered whether they often went to play in our meadow, and whether they might have seen anything that could give us any information about the identity of the body, but they said not.'

The Chief Inspector was not best pleased that the Rector had taken it upon himself to do a little amateur detective work; but as Parson's Close was his land, it was perhaps natural that he should be particularly concerned about what had happened.

'Well now, Mr Ainger: just a few questions, if you'll bear with me. The meadow where the body was found belongs to you in your capacity as Rector, doesn't it?'

'It's glebe land, part of my benefice as Rector of Breckham Market, yes.' Robin Ainger pushed his chair back from the kitchen table, crossed one long leg over the other and gave his attention to his empty plate. 'I can't dispose of the meadow in any way, but I obtain income from it. As you probably know, it's used as grazing land by the tenant of Church Farm.'

'And do you ever go into the meadow yourselves?'

They spoke simultaneously: 'No.'

'Never. I did think, when we first came,' added Gillian Ainger with a slightly self-conscious laugh, 'that I might sometimes go for walks there in the summer. But the cattle put me off. Bullocks are so inquisitive and pushy.'

'We rarely give a thought to the meadow,' said her husband. 'After all, it's across the road and behind palings, completely out of our sight.'

'So if anyone used it—children, or lovers, or blackberry pickers—you'd be unlikely to see them?'

'Most unlikely. Particularly if they got into the meadow at the lower end, from the by-pass.'

'Quite.' The Chief Inspector rose to go. 'Well, I'm obliged to you both for your help and hospitality.'

The telephone rang, and Mrs Ainger hurried to answer it. Her husband looked at his watch. 'I'm sorry if

I've kept you,' Quantrill went on. 'You both have meetings to go to, I believe.'

'Yes, school governors' for me, Mothers' Union for my wife. We're kept very busy.'

'So I see.' The phrase 'pillars of the community' came into Quantrill's head; Robin and Gillian Ainger were certainly that, by all accounts. He moved into the hall and put on his overcoat.

'Mr Quantrill!' said Ainger abruptly.

The Chief Inspector turned. Gillian had emerged from the study and the couple stood stiffly side by side.

'Yes, Mr Ainger?'

'Can you tell me what's happening? Have you discovered how the—the person died?'

'Oh, it's early days for that. But there was no obvious evidence on or near the body.'

'And the identity?'

'No idea. Inspector Colman agrees that it's male, and that it has been there for a matter of months rather than years, but he hasn't had time yet to make a detailed examination. With luck there'll be some means of identification in the clothing.' He paused at the door. 'There was one interesting detail, though: a ring on the left hand, a big silver knuckleduster, very unusual and noticeable. If we have to start asking round the town, that'll probably help to jog someone's memory.'

The Aingers neither spoke nor looked at one another but, unobserved by the Chief Inspector, their hands met behind their backs in an anguished clasp.

Quantrill smiled at Gillian, thanked them for their help, and wished them both good-day.

# Chapter 5

'DC Wigby! My office, if you please. When you've finished keeping fit.'

The snow had hampered Detective Constable Ian Wigby's resolve to get his weight down after Christmas, but now it had begun to clear he started every morning with a brisk trot round the station yard. Chief Inspector Quantrill had caught sight and sound of him as Wigby forged in through the side door, and had decided that he was the best available man for the Parson's Close investigation.

Wigby was thirty-two years old. He had been at Breckham Market for six years, and knew the town as well as anyone. He was noisy, cheerful and irreverent, but an experienced and competent detective with a magistrates' commendation to his credit. His methods, however, were suspect. 'You've got to know 'em to catch 'em,' was his motto, 'and you've got to mix with 'em to know 'em.' DC Wigby spent much of his working time in pubs, mingling with local villains and their hangers-on and picking up information. Sometimes he solved the crimes he worked on and sometimes, unaccountably, he failed. Nothing had ever been proved against him, but his colleagues were of the opinion that he did remarkably well to maintain his smart bungalow, his pretty, well-dressed wife and his two immaculately turned-out small daughters on a detective constable's pay. On the whole Quantrill liked him, but he did not entirely trust him.

DC Wigby barged into the Chief Inspector's office. He was of medium height, and beefy with it. His hair and eyebrows were a bristly blond. He wore a heavy white sweater and a pair of pale grey trousers with an aggressive red and green overcheck.

'And what can I do for you, sir?' he enquired breezily.

'You can do something about the skeleton that was found yesterday.'

'Aha—Boney the mystery man. It's a bit much, I reckon, to have strange corpses littering the town. Gives the place a bad name.'

'Quite. Forensic are still working on the cause of death, but I want you to find out if anything was known about him locally.' Quantrill picked up the pathologist's preliminary report. 'Male, height six foot two, aged between twenty and twenty-four. Death occurred seven to eight months ago—say July or August last year. He was wearing denim trousers and jacket and canvas shoes. There was nothing on or in the clothing to identify him, but he wore this ring on his left hand.'

The Chief Inspector placed on his desk a plastic envelope containing a massive silver ring, as heavily convoluted as the boss on a medieval shield.

DC Wigby picked it up and whistled. 'If I'd seen him going to a football match in this thing, I'd have done him for wearing an offensive weapon.'

'Exactly—it's noticeable, so if he was in the town last summer the chances are that someone may remember having seen him.'

Wigby looked doubtful, but he answered cheerfully. 'Right. I'll ask around, then.'

'Do that. Of course, he may have no connection at all

with Breckham. I've asked for a computer run-through on the missing persons register, so we should get a lead from that; if we don't, we'll put out a public appeal. But you may get to hear of something this morning. There's a paragraph in the *Daily Press*, so it's bound to be a talking point in the town.'

'Thirsty work, talking,' observed Wigby with happy anticipation.

'Since you mention it,' said Quantrill, 'thanks: you can bring me a cup of coffee before you go.'

It was not often that Detective Constable Wigby received direct encouragement from the Chief Inspector to tour the pubs, and he meant to make the most of it. But first, because they weren't open before half-past ten, he drove along the main Yarchester road, on to the round-about and along the by-pass.

On his left was the conscientious mix of housing estates and schools and community buildings and factories and warehouses that formed the new town, the planners' Utopia where over half the crimes in the entire police division were committed out of boredom and a sense of alienation. On his right, rising up towards the church, was the muddle of the old town. This was the back view of Breckham Market, exposed by the building of the by-pass. Immediately after the roundabout, but with no access except from the town centre, was the poorest quarter, a cluster of dingy red brick walls and slated roofs known officially as Sebastopol Street and generally as Duck End. Further along the by-pass lay the allotment gardens; past the hedged-in allotments was Parson's Close.

Wigby stopped his car on the verge, behind a police

van. He got out. It was still bitterly cold, and four uni-
formed policemen were engaged on the numbing task of
scraping away snow from the grass at the lower end of the
meadow, in the hope of bringing something significant to
light. Wigby grinned to himself, turned up the dark fur
collar of his sheepskin jacket and—having served in the
Royal Marines before he joined the police force—assessed
the area with a practised military eye.

On the far side of Parson's Close was an electricity
substation, separated from the meadow by a high wire
security fence. Access to Parson's Close could therefore
be gained from three sides only: across the barbed wire
from the bypass at the lower end, from St Botolph Street
at the top, or through the allotment hedge at the side. The
allotments were still under snow, their makeshift huts giving them the look of an abandoned refugee camp, their
footpaths invisible; but Wigby knew that the paths were
there, and that one of them connected Parson's Close
with Duck End. The street and the meadow were no more
than a hundred yards apart.

If the man's body had been brought along the by-pass
and dumped, that was not Wigby's immediate concern.
But if he had entered Parson's Close alive last summer,
either from St Botolph's or from Duck End by way of the
allotments, then, Wigby calculated, somebody local had
probably seen him.

There were no pubs in St Botolph's, but in Duck End
there was the Maltster's Arms. Wigby turned his car,
drove back to the roundabout, and took the narrow road
that led directly into the old town. He reached Duck End
with a minute to spare before opening time.

Sebastopol Street, built by a brewer named Gosling in
the middle years of the nineteenth century, had long since
been declared unfit for human habitation. Many of the

houses were empty, their doors and windows boarded up, but the remainder were inhabited by elderly owner-occu-piers who eked out their lives there, plagued by cock-roaches and damp and rheumatism. Smoke rose from their chimneys, and fire-ash lay pink on the snow outside their doors so as to give the residents a firmer footing when they ventured outside.

As Wigby approached the door of the Maltster's Arms, the bolts were being drawn. 'Morning, Mrs Phelps,' he said jovially to the landlady.

Alice Enid Phelps, licensed to sell beer, wines and spirits to be consumed on or off the premises, gave him a narrow stare. She was small and thin and grey, but her eyes were as sharp as her tongue.

'I know you,' she said. 'You're that policeman who came here upsetting my customers.'

'That was eighteen months ago,' Wigby protested.

'I never forget a face.'

She was in her middle sixties, a widow who had applied for the licence to be transferred to her after her husband's death not because she drank or enjoyed com-pany, but because the pub was both her home and her livelihood. The local brewery had been closed for thirty years and so the pub was a free house which, within the licensing laws, she ruled as she pleased.

'The last time you came nosing round here,' she continued, keeping him on the doorstep, 'was when you were looking for poor old Mrs Bedingfield's Reggie's Kevin. But he wasn't the one you were after, because he's going straight. His Granny would never have had him to live with her otherwise, because this is a respectable neighbourhood, and I keep a respectable house and I want no policemen poking about here and upsetting my customers. What do you want, anyway?'

Wigby blinked at her, moon-faced with assumed innocence. 'I was hoping for a Guinness, and a bit of a warm-up. I've been on duty in Parson's Close ever since daylight, and it's stingy old weather out there.'

'I keep no Guinness,' she said. 'There's no call for it in Duck End.'

'Mild, then?' suggested Wigby. 'A half would go down well.'

She allowed him, grudgingly, into the only bar. It was a cheerless room, the wallpaper yellow with age and tide-marked with rising damp, the paintwork brown, the wooden settles as unwelcoming as chapel pews. Mrs Phelps's only concession to her customers' comfort was a small fire that oozed smoke from between the bars of a narrow Victorian grate.

'Ah, that's better.' Wigby welcomed it with exaggerated, hand-toasting enthusiasm. 'That's what I needed, after searching Parson's Close.'

Mrs Phelps failed either to soften or to rise to his hint. She drew his beer, took his money and kept her mouth tight.

''Spect you've heard about the skeleton,' he prompted.

'Yes. But it's nobody from hereabouts, that I do know. And there's nothing any of my customers can tell you about it, so you're wasting your time.'

'You keep a good drop of beer, though,' he told her.

Mrs Phelps seemed not entirely displeased. 'Well, you must stay if you want, I suppose. But I'll thank you to keep yourself to yourself. And don't sit near the fire, neither.'

Wigby removed himself to a draughty bar stool, and watched as the seats at the table near the fire slowly filled up with regulars. There were half a dozen of them, old men in cloth caps and woollen scarves and layers of waistcoats and jackets and overcoats. They greeted the landlady respectfully as they crept in, and she replied with a nod and their names, at the same time drawing half a pint of their preferred drink and wordlessly exchanging it for their money.

The old men's morning ritual unfolded, beginning with talk of the weather and of the deaths that had been announced in that day's local paper. DC Wigby, who had been given some wary glances at first, leaned silently on the bar and stared out of the window at a corner shop that had been closed for so long that it still bore on its walls a battered tin advertisement with the message, *Rinso saves coal on washdays.*

Eventually the conversation turned to the discovery of the skeleton, but it seemed to arouse no great interest. The residents of Duck End were too old to be concerned with anything that did not touch their own lives. They knew that the bones were not those of a local man, and apart from expressing a certain amount of indignation that a stranger should choose Breckham Market to die in, they had little to say on the subject. One of them opened a box of dominoes, and they settled down to concentrate on their pastime.

Wigby was about to drink up and go when the door opened again and another man came in, a hale sixty-five-year-old wearing a flat cap and a short motoring coat, but with cycle clips on his trousers.

'Why, it's the boy Walter!' said one of the old men, and the atmosphere immediately brightened. Even Mrs Phelps permitted herself a smile of welcome. There was a good deal of chaffing, with the men addressing each other in the East Anglian way as 'Bor'.

The boy Walter, DC Wigby gathered, rented one of the allotments at the back of Duck End; born and brought up in the street, he now lived near the railway station. Evidently he made the Maltster's Arms his headquarters during the gardening season, and liked to drop in occasionally during the winter. The bad weather had kept him away for weeks, and the regulars hailed him as the promise of spring.

If Walter cycled from his home to his allotment, reasoned Wigby, visualizing the layout of the town, he probably approached the allotments from St Botolph Street, at the top end of Parson's Close. He could be a useful man to talk to. Wigby sat tight, and bought a packet of peanuts to justify his continuing presence.

Having greeted the old men individually, the boy Walter left them to their dominoes and went to the bar. He was a pensioner of a different generation, alert, well-fed, immensely good humoured; but Wigby knew better than to attempt to rush a Suffolk man by offering to buy him a drink before they had become acquainted.

The detective waited until Walter had bought his own beer, and Mrs Phelps had retired to the back room, and then he gave the man a friendly nod: ''Morning.'

Walter was non-committal: 'How do.'

'Real brass monkey weather, still.'

This time Walter grinned. 'Ar, that is. Better for getting about, though. First time I've been on the bike since afore Christmas.'

'Do you come along St Botolph's?'

'Not today, not with snow on the 'lotments. Generally I do, though. Ar, I wouldn't mind a pound note for every time I've biked along there.'

Wigby knew that the expression was nothing more than a confirmation of the man's acquaintance with the area; Walter would have been astonished and offended to be offered money. Instead, Wigby showed him his warrant card. 'You've heard about the skeleton in Parson's Close, I suppose,' he asked.

Walter nodded, his eyes rounding with interest. 'How did that come to be there?' he demanded.

'That's what I'm trying to find out. For a start, I want to know who it was. We know it was a tall chap, early twenties, died last summer. He wore a big silver ring on his left hand. Can you remember if you saw anyone like that, on your way to or from your allotment?'

Walter shook his head slowly. 'I don't recall seeing anybody—any stranger, that is. There was a tent, though, in Parson's Close last summer. Just one, a little orange thing, up near the trees. You couldn't see it from St Botolph's because of the fence, but I saw it from my 'lotment. I thought it must belong to the Australian.'

'What Australian?'

'Why, the one with the car. I didn't ever see anybody in it, but the car was parked along St Botolph's at the top end of Parson's Close most of the time in the early part of last summer. It was a Jap car, a Datsun like my son's, but there was a sticker saying *Australia* in the back window.'

'Did you notice the number of the car? Or any part of the number?'

Walter pushed back his cap and scratched the top of his greying head. 'No, I didn't take that much interest. I knew it was a Datsun from the shape, same as my son's. His'n's yellow, though. This one was red.'

'And it was there in the early part of the summer, you say?'

'Ar. I noticed it first in April, time I was putting in my peas. It was parked there on and off for a month or two, and then it seemed to be there all the time until we went on our holiday.'

'When was that?'

'Beginning of August. Me and the missus go to a caravan at Yarmouth with my daughter and her family for the first full week in August every year. We got back home on the Saturday and I biked up to the 'lotment after tea, just to see how everything was doing. And I remember noticing that the car wasn't there, nor yet the tent. I never saw the car or the tent after that.'

# Chapter 6

**W**igby bought the boy Walter a beer, and left. He drove into the centre of the town and went to one of his regular pubs, the Boot, for a small Guinness to wash down the Maltster's peanuts. There was a good deal of speculation in the bar about the identity of the Parson's Close skeleton, but no one had met or heard of an Australian in the town the previous summer. Wigby moved on, this time walking up to St Botolph's parish hall, just behind the church. He had been there the previous day, when he made the initial investigation of the damage that had been done at the youth club meeting.

''Morning, Mr Blore. How's it going?'

The caretaker of the hall, who was also the verger of the church, was a thin man in a zippered fawn cardigan, with mournful eyes and an anxiously neat moustache. He switched off his electric floor polisher and showed the detective constable what he had done to make the hall usable.

'As you see, I'm getting the place clean and straight. But as for the actual damage...' Heartbroken, he gestured to the shattered windows that he had blocked with hardboard, the broken legs of the table tennis table, the smashed stereo speakers. 'It's the *waste* of it all, Mr Wigby, the wicked waste...'

Wigby commiserated with him and agreed with his strictures on the irresponsibility of youth, although he personally believed it to be a natural and healthy state. He was proud of having once been a holy terror. In his opinion, a boy who had never had the guts to buck authority would be too spineless to make an effective copper; and a boy who hadn't got the sense to conceal his misdemeanours wouldn't know how to start being a detective.

'What I came to tell you,' Wigby said, interrupting the verger's woeful recital, 'is that a sergeant from Yarchester is coming to do the investigation. He'll be in to see you this afternoon. We can't do it ourselves—it's a bit awkward, with the DCI's boy belonging to the youth club.'

The verger nodded sadly. He led the way into the kitchen and switched on the electric kettle. 'I'd never have thought it of young Peter Quantrill, not with his Dad a Chief Inspector.'

'Doesn't matter who their Dads are,' snorted Wigby. 'Makes 'em worse, sometimes. Doesn't matter who anybody is, we're all human.'

Edgar Blore looked as though he would like to deny it, but Wigby led him on to the subject of the skeleton and asked whether he had seen either the tent in Parson's Close or the red Datsun with the *Australia* sticker in St Botolph's Street, the previous summer.

'A tent? That's news to me.' The verger picked up a damp-dry tea-bag from the saucer where he had parked it after an earlier brew-up, and made an insipid cup of tea. He offered it to Wigby, who declined it promptly.

'The Rector never said anything about anyone camping in the meadow,' went on Edgar Blore, returning the wrinkled corpse of the tea-bag to the saucer for further use, 'but then he might not know about it either. That's what I said to Mrs Blore this morning, when I read the piece in the paper: for all it's Parson's Close, anything could happen there without Mr Ainger's knowledge. It's my belief that the skeleton must have got there from the by-pass. It's nothing to do with Breckham at all.'

'What about the car, then?'

'To tell you the truth, Mr Wigby, I don't go along St Botolph's very often. I see the Rector a great deal, of course. This is a very busy parish and I try to help him as much as I can, but I usually see him either here or in the church. I try not to bother him at the Rectory, and when I do have to go there I've got too much on my mind to take any notice of parked cars.'

'Well then, did you see a stranger about here last summer?' Wigby began to describe the dead man, but the verger held up a mildly reproachful hand.

'Come, come, that's asking the impossible. We get no end of strangers visiting the church in the summer—we're a tourist attraction here at St Botolph's, you know. There's no time to take notice of what they look like.'

'What about what they sound like?' said Wigby. 'This man might have been Australian.'

'Australia, America, Scandinavia—they come from all over. No, I'm sorry, Mr Wigby, but I can't help you.' He rinsed out his cup, put it upside down on the drainer and looked at his watch. 'You must excuse me, but we've got a funeral at twelve. I must go and set out the bier.'

He moved away, and then remembered something. 'Wait a minute, though. There was an Australian *girl* about here last summer. A friend of Mrs Ainger. Spent a lot of time at the Rectory. Not that I saw her myself, except once in church, but my wife saw her several times. Mrs Blore helps at the Rectory two mornings a week, and she said that the girl lived there for most of July, before she went off on her travels again. Perhaps she had some connection with this man you're talking about.'

'It's worth following up. Thanks for the information, Mr Blore. We'll talk to Mrs Ainger, then.'

The verger looked worried, in a protective way. 'She'll be over in the new town today, at the community centre. It's one of her busiest days—but I think it would be more considerate if you were to see her there rather than at the Rectory. Mrs Blore and I often say that Mr and Mrs Ainger get no peace at home. There's always somebody bothering them about something, wanting them to witness wills or sign passport applications or give character references, and ninety per cent of them aren't even churchgoers.'

DC Wigby, one of the ninety per cent, went away well satisfied with the progress of his enquiries. He knew that the Chief Inspector was in touch with the Aingers, and would want to do the follow-up himself; but with a skeleton as subject, there was no need to report back in a hurry. The DCI had told him to find out what was being said in the town, and it was a pity to waste good drinking time. Wigby moved across the road to the Coney and Thistle, and ordered the other half of his Guinness.

The customers at the Coney had several improbable and ribald theories about the origin of the skeleton, but no one seemed to know anything about the tall man with the ring, the red Datsun or the tent in Parson's Close. Wigby congratulated himself on his strategy. He'd certainly ferreted out as much information as that jumped-up Sergeant Tait—an Inspector now, dammit—could have done, for all Tait's university and police college background. Experience was worth ten times more than paper qualifications and he, Wigby, had been a detective while Master Tait was still at school.

He finished his drink and returned to the station, anticipating Chief Inspector Quantrill's approval. But he was too late.

'The Rector's already been to see me,' said Quantrill. 'He came soon after you left this morning. He thinks the skeleton may belong to an Australian who camped on and off last summer in Parson's Close.'

'I've been wasting me time, then,' complained Wigby, crestfallen.

'Not the way it smells from here. Besides, you've told me a couple of interesting things the Rector didn't mention. We won't make any more enquiries until I've cleared them up with him, so you'll be free to brief Sergeant Tuckswood on the church hall incident as soon as he arrives from Yarchester. Give him whatever help he needs—short of driving for him. I don't want him going back to HQ saying that Breckham CID needs breathalyzing.'

The February sun was low and watery but at least it was doing its best, and for the first time since the snow had begun Chief Inspector Quantrill went out voluntarily, just before twelve, for an hour's walk through the town. It was something he always enjoyed: an opportunity to get away from his desk, to clear his head and to keep in touch with the everyday life of Breckham.

It was market day, and the town was busier than usual; certainly busier than it had been during the weeks of snow and ice, when the shoppers had been unable to come in from the surrounding villages. Cold as it still was, the contrast with the preceding weeks was so great that people paused in the streets to chat as though it were spring. The main roads and pavements were clear, although wet and dirty, but the grey remains of the snow still blocked the gutters.

The funeral bell was tolling as Quantrill passed the church, its muffled clang sounding out high above the market place while the buying and selling and talking and chaffing, and the frying and munching at the fish-and-chip van, went on exactly as usual. This higgledy-piggledy juxtaposition of church and market was a part of country town living that he particularly valued: the in-the-midst-of-death-we-are-in-life factor that reminded people of their own mortality but prevented them from being permanently overawed by the inevitability of it.

He edged across the market place through a narrow passage between crates of cabbage and a rail of outsize crimplene dresses in pastel colours, and then stood for a few moments with his back to the massive oak corner post of the medieval Coney and Thistle, observing the scene. The church was just across the road, rising high from its walled churchyard in which the ground had been lifted by generations of unmarked burials. A cemetery had been established on the outskirts of the town in the late nineteenth century, and so St Botolph's churchyard, no longer used, was still white with untouched snow.

The clock in the Victorian Italianate tower of the town hall on the other side of the market place struck twelve, and the Rector emerged from the south porch of St Botolph's and strode down the well-swept path to the gate to await the arrival of the hearse. Robin Ainger looked almost improperly youthful and handsome in his vestments. There was something about him that worried the Chief Inspector considerably. Not his appearance: Quantrill was not so intemperately Nonconformist by upbringing that he imagined that real-life Anglican parsons ought to be, like television comedy stereotypes, either amiably absent-minded elderly men or well-meaning young buffoons. What bothered him about Ainger was the probability that he had failed to admit the true extent of his knowledge of the corpse in Parson's Close.

What Ainger had told him was extremely helpful, and apparently complete. Quantrill would have accepted it—had, at first, accepted it—without hesitation. But then DC Wigby had turned up with further information that was surely relevant, although the Rector had not mentioned it. Quantrill had given him ample opportunity. *Is there anything else you can tell me, Mr Ainger?* he had asked. *Anything at all that you think might help us to find out how the man came to die?* And the Rector had looked at him with blank eyes and had said, *No.*

The volume of market noise lessened slightly and the Chief Inspector turned his head to see the town's traffic warden, magisterial in dark uniform and yellow capband, stopping both traffic and pedestrians to allow the funeral cortège along the narrow street that separated the market stalls from the churchyard. Quantrill took off his hat and stood for a moment with his head bared while the hearse passed. He saw it stop at the churchyard-gate. The Rector stepped forward.

From across the road, the Chief Inspector stared speculatively at the Reverend Robin Ainger. A priest, and a pillar of the community; but for all that, a man like any other.

The savoury smell of fish fried in batter drifted across from the busy van. 'And the next?' shouted the man behind the serving hatch as he slapped a steaming parcel in front of a customer. Quantrill turned and made his way into the Coney and Thistle for a pint of Adnams bitter and an early lunch.

# Chapter 7

It was ridiculous that he missed Martin Tait so much. There had been so many occasions, during the year they'd worked together, when he had longed to see the back of the cocksure young detective sergeant. But although the two men had often disagreed, their discussions had served to keep Quantrill mentally at full stretch. They had often met for a working lunch at the Coney, and the Chief Inspector wished that Tait were there now.

Ian Wigby could never be an adequate substitute. He had done a very useful piece of enquiry work that morning, and Quantrill intended to bear in mind that he deserved a Guinness for it; but the detective constable's limitations were those of the Chief Inspector himself.

Like Quantrill, Wigby was a Suffolk man by birth and upbringing. He could go about the division extracting information from local people without arousing either suspicion or resentment—something that Martin Tait, with his sharply elegant clothes and his expensively educated voice, had never been able to do. But Quantrill knew that neither he himself nor Wigby would be able to get into sufficiently close conversation with the Reverend Robin Ainger to find out what motivated him. Martin Tait would have been the ideal man for that particular job.

The bar at the Coney was busy. Quantrill ordered

and paid for the hot dish of the day, exchanged a word with some acquaintances, and then carried his mug of beer up two worn stone steps and into the heavily beamed snug, where he found an empty table by one of the windows.

A girl with a dark pony-tail of hair and a striped butcher's apron over her jeans brought in a knife and fork rolled in a paper napkin, and a plate of home-made steak and mushroom pie. Quantrill began the meal with a good appetite, tempted by the smell of the gravy that oozed out as he cut into the golden crust, but his intake soon slackened as he went over in his mind the conversation he had had that morning with Robin Ainger.

The Rector's unexpected arrival in the front office had been announced by the desk sergeant, who assumed that the visit was in connection with young Peter Quantrill's alleged misdeeds and tried to convey over the intercom that he was ready, if required, to close ranks in sympathy. The Chief Inspector, making the same assumption, had suppressed a sigh and gone to the top of the stairs to meet the Rector, sending the escorting police cadet down again to fetch some coffee. But Robin Ainger was clutching a copy of the local newspaper, and he began to say what was on his mind before Quantrill could invite him to take off his duffle coat and sit down.

'This body—the skeleton in the Close. Gillian and I have read the report and talked it over, and we think we now know who it might be.'

'You do? Good, that'll be a great help.'

Ainger had looked anxiously determined as he came in, but the determination seemed to slide off with his coat, leaving only the anxiety. Quantrill had to say, 'Yes, Mr Ainger?' encouragingly to persuade him to continue.

'I don't *know*, of course,' Ainger said. 'I may be completely wrong, and wasting your time. But a young man camped in Parson's Close for some weeks last summer—an Australian. His name was Athol Garrity, and I think he said that he came from Brisbane. We didn't see him often, and he didn't let us know that he was leaving, but we definitely didn't see him after the beginning of August.'

Quantrill took from the drawer of his desk the plastic envelope containing the big silver ring. 'Do you happen to recognize this?'

Ainger glanced at it. The whites of his eyes were dull, the blue irises so pale above his clerical grey that they looked almost drained. 'Ah yes—you mentioned a ring when you came to see us. My wife remembered, after you'd gone, that Garrity wore one on his left hand. That was what made us think that the body could be his. I can't, of course, be positive that this is the same ring—'

'No, no. But your information is extremely helpful. We'll pass it on to the Australian authorities and ask them to have Garrity's dental records sent over. If the skeleton is his, it can be identified by the teeth. I'm much obliged to you for coming forward so quickly, Mr Ainger. It'll save my men from tramping about the town making enquiries.'

'That's what I thought.' Robin Ainger rose to go, just as a policewoman brought in a tray of coffee. WPC Patsy Hopkins, who had a requited admiration for Douglas Quantrill, had heard from the desk sergeant that he was being grilled by the Rector about his son's behaviour. She had intercepted the cadet who was about to carry two slopped-over cups of canteen coffee into the Chief Inspector's office, and in an act of loyalty and affection had substituted one cup made from her own private jar of freeze-dried coffee granules. She carried in the tray herself to ensure that Quantrill got the right cup. Breckham Market police believed in looking after their own.

'Don't go, please, Mr Ainger,' said Quantrill. 'That is, if you can spare me a few more minutes. I'd like to know as much as I can—many thanks, Patsy—about this Australian.'

'There's not much I can tell you,' said Ainger, sitting down again with some reluctance. 'He said that he was backpacking round the world, and spending six months in England. When he disappeared, we naturally assumed that he'd moved on.'

'What brought him to Breckham in the first place?'

'Apparently he'd been staying with a student friend at Yarchester, and he came over to look at the monumental brasses in St Botolph's. They're famous, as you probably know. I happened to see him in the church one day last May, and he asked me whether he could take some rubbings of the brasses. He also mentioned that he was looking for somewhere to pitch his tent for the summer—a base camp from which he could make a few assaults on London, as he put it—and I said that he could use Parson's Close.'

Quantrill scratched his chin. 'You mentioned yesterday that there were cattle there. Cattle and campers don't usually mix.'

Ainger hesitated. 'Ah, yes. Well, actually, there weren't any cattle there last summer. The farmer decided that it was anachronistic to drive them through the town twice a year, and gave up the tenancy. But there's water for the cattle—a standpipe and trough at the lower end of the meadow—so it's ideal for camping.'

'I see. Was he on his own?'

'He travelled alone, as far as I know.'

'And how did he travel?'

'Hitching lifts, I imagine. Or possibly he went to London by train. I really don't know, Mr Quantrill. As I said, we saw very little of him.'

'You've said *we*, Mr Ainger. So presumably your wife met him too?'

'Yes—yes, he called at the Rectory when he first came to the town, and we gave him a meal. But he was never more than a casual acquaintance, and we had no idea how he spent his time. As you know, we can't see the meadow from the Rectory, so we knew nothing of his comings and goings.'

'You're being extremely helpful,' Quantrill encouraged him. 'What we want now is to talk to someone who knew him well. Did he tell you who the student friend in Yarchester was?'

'Another Australian, I believe. All the people he knew seemed to be transients, like himself.'

'Very probably. Now, can you possibly pin down for me the last date on which you saw him?'

Ainger laced his fingers together and addressed them slowly. 'I went away for a few days' break last August, from the first to the 6th. I definitely didn't see Garrity after I returned. My wife was at home, but she is sure that she didn't see him during that time. We've discussed it carefully, and we think that we both saw him for the last time about two days before I went away—say the 29th of July.'

'And what was he doing when you saw him?'

There was a long pause. Then Ainger said, 'He was in St Botolph's, heading for the gate into Parson's Close. He was drunk. And not for the first time.'

'Ah.' Quantrill grinned. 'I got the impression, Mr Ainger, that you didn't much like the man. That was why, was it?'

The Rector struggled with his evident disinclination to speak ill of the dead. 'We certainly didn't find him a desirable guest. He was—well, frankly, uncouth. Gillian and I avoided him whenever we could, and we were not at all sorry when we didn't see him again.'

'Understandably. And it's very useful for us to know about his drinking. It may help to account for his death.'

'You don't yet know how he died?'

'Not so far. The coroner opens his inquest on Monday, and no doubt he'll adjourn it until the Australian authorities have had time to confirm the identification. By then the forensic science people should be able to tell us their findings. In the meantime I'll follow up your information so that we can give the coroner as complete a picture as possible. Now, is there anything else that you can tell me, Mr Ainger? Anything at all that you think might help us to find out more about the man, and how he came to die?'

And that was when the Reverend Robin Ainger had looked at the Chief Inspector with pale, blank eyes, and had said, 'No.'

The Rector was lying, Quantrill decided as he finished his steak and mushroom pie. Not necessarily lying in any of the details he had given, but certainly omitting to tell the facts in full; and, yes, lying when he had said there was nothing else he could tell the police.

What about the car with the *Australia* sticker that had been seen parked along St Botolph's Street last summer? What about the Australian girl who had been a frequent visitor to the Rectory, even living there during July? There had to be some connection between the girl and the car and the dead man. The girl was the obvious person to help the police with their enquiries, and Ainger must know her name. So why had he deliberately withheld that information? Was it because he knew more about the corpse in Parson's Close than he cared to admit?

Quantrill pushed aside his plate and lifted his mug. He glanced out of the window. The mourners were coming out of St Botolph's after the funeral service, and the traffic warden was organizing the departure of the hearse and the accompanying cars. The Rector had presumably gone ahead so as to reach the cemetery first. Quantrill couldn't see him; instead, he saw the Rector's wife.

Gillian Ainger was just outside the Coney, buying from a vegetable stall, a preoccupied frown on her face and a laden shopping-bag in her hand. Quantrill thought rapidly. He had really wanted to challenge Robin Ainger about the Australian girl; he wanted to hear not only what Ainger said about her, but the way he said it. However, the girl had been Mrs Ainger's friend, according to the verger, and so it was possibly more appropriate to make the initial approach to her. He could always tackle her husband later.

He seized his hat and overcoat, and caught up with her outside Boots the chemist. 'Good morning, Mrs Ainger. I wonder if you could spare me a few minutes of your time?' It would have been civil to invite her to join him for a drink, but she looked too harassed to want to linger.

'Oh—Mr Quantrill...' She was evidently taken aback, and not in any way glad to see him. 'I'm afraid... I really must ask you to excuse me. This is my day for helping at the community centre on the new estate. I slipped away to do some shopping and make Dad's lunch, but I have to get back as soon as possible.'

'I won't delay you, I promise. Perhaps I could walk

back to the Rectory with you, if you've finished your shopping? Here, let me carry that.'

He insisted on taking from her hand the bulging shopping-bag with its leafy protrusion of cabbage and celery. She seemed inordinately embarrassed, whether by his company or by the fact that he was carrying her shopping he wasn't sure.

His stride, which he had shortened to Mrs Ainger's, checked as he caught sight of his own wife disappearing into the butcher's. He hated helping her with the shopping, and always tried to make his irregular working hours an excuse for not doing so. He'd never live it down if she were to see him now, carrying another woman's shopping-bag...

He jammed his hat over his eyes and rounded the comer into St Botolph's Street in a hurry. Gillian Ainger had to trot to keep up with him, doing a skip and a jump to avoid wading through the dirty slush in the gutter.

'Have you—did my husband come to see you this morning?' she asked a little breathlessly.

He slowed his pace. 'Yes, he told me about the Australian who camped in Parson's Close last summer. It's a very useful lead. What I'd really like to do now is to talk to someone who knew him better than your husband and yourself. Is there anyone you can suggest?'

After a moment's hesitation she said, 'No. I'm afraid not.'

He turned his head to look at her. Vanity-free, she had bundled up her fair hair under a woollen hat, but fine tendrils of it had escaped untidily over her ears and at the nape of her neck. If she had put on any make-up that morning, it had worn off. She was pale, apart from the tip of her nose which was pink with cold. Her knee-length boots were shabby and she walked with her chin

tucked into the yellowed fleece of a long-service sheepskin coat.

Then, conscious of his gaze, she raised her head and
looked at him. Her cheeks coloured suddenly, redder than
her nose, but she said nothing more.

'Whose was the car, Mrs Ainger?' he asked her gently.
'We've been making enquiries, you see, and I know that a
red Datsun car with an *Australia* sticker in the rear win-
dow was often parked in St Botolph's Street last summer.
But when your husband and I were talking about Athol
Garrity's comings and goings, he didn't mention it.'

She lifted her chin. 'There was no reason why he
should. The car wasn't Athol's. It belonged to another
Australian, a friend of mine, Janey Rolph. She didn't like
Athol, and as far as I know she never even gave him a
ride. If my husband didn't mention the car, that was why.
It didn't seem relevant.'

'I'd have been glad if he'd told me about the girl,
though. As I said, we need to talk to someone who knew
Garrity.'

'But Janey's no longer in this country. That would be
why Robin didn't tell you about her. She was doing a
post-graduate course at the university, at Yarchester.
She'd finished her thesis, and she left the country at the
end of July.'

'That doesn't prevent us from having her questioned,
if we need to. We can get her home address from the
university.'

Gillian Ainger gave him a startled look, as though that
possibility had never occurred to her. Then she said, 'But
Janey wasn't going back to Australia. She was moving on
to the United States.'

'Do you know where she is now?'

'No. No, I haven't heard from her since she left.'

Her chin was tucked into the collar of her coat again, but Quantrill could see a tightening of the muscles at the side of her jaw.

'What was Janey Rolph's relationship with Garrity?' he asked.

'They originated from the same small town, somewhere near Brisbane. Athol looked her up, in Yarchester, when he came to this country, and scrounged a bed space in her room.'

'Were they lovers?'

'Good heavens no! I told you, Janey didn't like him. She felt a kind of home-town obligation to him, that's all.'

'Tell me about her?' Quantrill suggested.

She was obviously reluctant to do so. 'There's not a great deal to tell. We met by chance last spring, and I invited her to visit us. She came quite often after that. She was twenty-two, and homesick, and I enjoyed her company.' She looked as though she was about to add something, then decided against it.

'I heard that she stayed with you for most of July.'

Gillian's head came round with a jerk. She reddened again, but her voice stayed level. 'Yes, she did. I imagine that was why Athol came here. He said that he was interested in brass-rubbing, but I think that he'd lost the roof over his head when Janey moved out of her room, and he was really looking for somewhere to pitch his tent.'

'And did they spend much time together while they were both in Breckham?'

'Virtually none. Janey avoided him whenever she could. She spent her time with us, finishing her thesis. Goodness knows what Athol did—he came and went as he pleased, and we rarely saw him or knew whether he was still in Breckham. Or cared, quite frankly. He was probably out drinking most of the time.'

Their slow walk through the remains of the snow had carried them along the length of the old churchyard, and the walled Rectory garden. They had reached the gate to the drive and Gillian Ainger stood fidgeting with the latch, obviously anxious to go indoors and get on with her busy life.

'You say that Janey Rolph left the country at the end of July. When, exactly?'

'She drove down to London on the 30th, as far as I can remember.'

'And you last saw Athol Garrity on the 29th. Hasn't it struck you as odd, Mrs Ainger, that her departure should coincide with his death?'

Gillian Ainger stood back and looked him straight in the eye. 'The date of Janey's departure had been fixed for months. She was in England on a student's permit that expired at the end of July. But Athol's movements were unpredictable, as I've already told you.'

'It's still an interesting coincidence.'

'What coincidence are you talking about, Mr Quantrill?' Her voice began to shake with indignant reproach. 'I think you're trying to take advantage of me to push me into some kind of premature speculation. Have you been able to establish the date of death of the body you've found? Have you established whether it really is Athol Garrity's? Because if you haven't...'

She stopped, aware that she was becoming shrill; she drew a deep breath, and spoke with firm resolution. 'The Rector and I have tried to help you as much as possible, Mr Quantrill. We've given you as much information as we can and I really think—don't you?—that it would be as well if you established your facts before questioning either of us any further.'

The strength of her reply took the Chief Inspector by

surprise. He stood discomfited, recalling that his son was currently suspected of taking part in a particularly senseless act of vandalism on church property, and that the Rector's wife knew all about it. He remembered too that the detective sergeant from Yarchester who was dealing with the enquiry was coming that evening to interview Peter at home in front of his parents.

Quantrill found that he had nothing more to say. He handed over the shopping-bag, lifted his hat, and skulked off.

# Chapter 8

'Kids...' thought Douglas Quantrill sourly, twenty-four hours later. Had he been king that day, he would have banished from Breckham Market everyone under the age of eighteen. Boys especially. His own, to start with.

It was not only Peter's behaviour—half childishly defensive, half truculent—in front of Sergeant Tuckswood the previous evening that irked him. Quantrill had earlier, during the course of the afternoon, gone with DC Wigby to talk to the two boys who had found the skeleton, and their righteous evasions had left him suspicious and frustrated.

Justin Muttock and Adrian Orris were having an unforgettable half-term holiday. Their discovery had initially terrified them, but as soon as they had unloaded the responsibility of it on to the nearest adult they began to recover. Before long, they thought themselves heroes: taken home in a police car, listened to respectfully by a note-taking constable, cosseted first by Justin's grandmother and then by their parents, talked to matily by the Rector, and finally visited by a reporter and a photographer from the *East Anglian Daily Press*.

Their photographs had appeared on the front page of the newspaper on the day of Quantrill's visit. Justin's

Gran, who was a school dinner-lady and therefore available during the holidays to mind the two boys while their mothers worked at the egg-packing depot, had immediately rushed out to have her hair done, in the hope that a television reporter would soon be on his way to her terraced house in Victoria Road.

Mrs Muttock senior was in her early fifties, a short, round, perkily youthful grandmother; her hair had required only a little assistance to restore its natural darkness, and when Quantrill and Wigby arrived she was wearing a skittish skirt and rather a lot of eye-shadow and lipstick. She had been wearing it all day, to the sardonic amusement of her neighbours, and had still not given up hope that an Anglia Television van might at any moment come into view. Two plain-clothes policemen were an unsatisfactory substitute; but her neighbours were not to know that unless she revealed it by her demeanour on the doorstep, and so she greeted the men with considerably more enthusiasm than they were accustomed to.

The boys, having told their brief story so often the previous day, had become blasé. Justin's Gran had forbidden them to go out, in case the Anglia van should come, and so they were sprawled on the sitting-room floor playing a television game, an electronic ping-pong. DC Wigby joined them for a few noisy minutes while Mrs Muttock made a pot of tea, and then she switched off the set and Quantrill addressed the boys heartily.

'I expect the two of you often play in Parson's Close?'

Justin and Adrian glanced at each other. They were healthy and bright, tough in jeans and miniature army sweaters, but dutifully wearing slippers so as not to clump about on Justin's Gran's fitted carpet. They exuded innocence, but the look they exchanged had counselled caution.

Adrian, the elder, cleared his throat. 'Oh no,' he said virtuously. 'It's private—it says so on the gate.'

Quantrill tried to reassure them. 'I never let a thing like that stop me when I was a boy,' he said with heavy jollity.

They stared at him with total disbelief, as though they imagined he had been born that age and size. Quantrill tried again, thinking they might find it easier to imagine Ian Wigby at junior school: 'And as for the constable here, he was always up to mischief.'

'A young monkey, I was,' agreed Wigby. 'Nothing really wrong, mind,' he added responsibly, 'but generally naughty.'

Mrs Muttock senior fluttered her mascara'd eyelashes at the detective constable over her teacup. 'You were a proper little devil, I can tell that,' she said with admiration.

'The point is,' said Quantrill, ignoring her contribution, 'that if we'd wanted to play in Parson's Close when we were boys, we wouldn't have worried about a *Private* notice. *Private*,' he explained, 'means that you have no business to be there. You'll get into trouble with the owner if he catches you, and quite right too. But it isn't against the law. As long as you don't do any damage, it's no concern of the police.'

'But we don't want to go into Parson's Close,' said Justin. 'We only went there yesterday because of the snow. We always play in Castle Meadow, don't we, Adrian?' He reached up to the table for a cellophane packet of savoury snacks. A lurid red and green monster was printed on the packet. Weird green lettering, dripping red to represent blood, announced that the bag contained monster food. The creature's jaws drooled green saliva, and in its talons it grasped a thigh bone.

Mrs Muttock senior leaned over to poke DC Wigby in the ribs. 'Did you ever?' she demanded, half amused, half shocked. 'It beats me how they can fancy that stuff, after they've found a skellington. Poor little dears...' Unconcerned, the boys began to munch the contents of the packet, which looked and smelled like bone-shaped fragments of polyurethane fried in vegetable oil.

'Parson's Close,' said Quantrill firmly, trying to retain control of the interview. 'We know that a man camped there last summer. He had a small orange tent, and he pitched it somewhere up near the trees. Now, what I'd like to know is whether either of you boys saw that man, at any time during the summer—saw him, or spoke to him, or heard him speaking to anyone else?'

Justin and Adrian glanced sideways at each other, and then looked at the Chief Inspector over their monster food, with hugely guileless eyes.

'We always play in Castle Meadow,' said Adrian.

'We don't go into Parson's Close,' said Justin. 'It's private, you see,' he explained, as though to a couple of retarded eight-year-olds.

The policemen elected to drain their teacups and retire in good order. Mrs Muttock went with them to the front door.

'There's a chance that the boys may remember something that could be useful,' Quantrill told her. 'If you do hear them saying anything about Parson's Close, I'd be much obliged if you'd give DC Wigby a ring at the station.'

Mrs Muttock brightened, glad that her brief importance was not yet at an end. Wigby had just pulled on his coat, and she stepped forward to settle the dark fleecy collar for him. 'Definitely,' she said with fervour.

Alarmed, Wigby bolted down the snow-fringed concrete path. Quantrill thanked her for the tea and had begun to follow, when she called to him.

'I say—'

He returned to her side, thinking that this might be an equivalent of what he had heard described as the 'By the way, Doctor' syndrome. He felt certain that the boys were concealing something; they were too virtuous by half. Probably Justin's grandmother had a shrewd idea of what it might be, but found it difficult to express.

'Yes, Mrs Muttock?' he encouraged her.

But all she had wanted was to give her neighbours the maximum opportunity of seeing her in conversation with a tall dark stranger. She put her hand on his sleeve and motioned with her head towards the window of the sitting room.

'Monster food—did you ever! Funny little devils, kids, eh?' she said proudly.

Quantrill had agreed, but with no paternal pride. And then he had gone home to wait with his family for Peter's interview with Detective Sergeant Tuckswood.

He had said very little to his son since the previous morning, when the Rector had told him about Peter's possible involvement in the church-hall incident. It was a severe embarrassment, exacerbated by Molly's impartial reproaches to her husband on behalf of her son, and to her son on behalf of his father. She kept trying to talk it over, but all Quantrill would say to either of them was that Peter must tell the truth when Sergeant Tuckswood questioned him.

It had been difficult, while they waited for the Sergeant to come, to think of a suitable topic of conversation.

Fifteen-year-old Peter had grown rapidly during the previous six months, and in doing so he seemed to have sloughed off all his former interests. His mother was of the frequently voiced opinion that he had outgrown his strength, but his father silently suspected that he was bone idle.

Peter didn't believe in standing when he could sit, or sitting when he could lie down. He was waiting for the interview in a semi-recumbent position in a deep armchair, with his sneakered size tens resting on the coffee table. When his father joined him in the sitting-room Peter grudgingly, but without being told, acknowledged his presence by removing his feet from the table. After that the two of them sat on opposite sides of the room, listening to Molly making agitated noises with pots and pans in the kitchen.

Presently Quantrill cleared his throat. 'Did you hear about the skeleton that's been found in Parson's Close?' he asked socially.

'Mm,' said Peter. Had he been wearing a hat, he would have tipped it over his face to indicate that he was not at home; as it was, he made do with closing his eyes and scraping his dark fringe as low as possible with his fingers.

'We think it might have been an Australian who camped in the meadow last summer.'

'Umph,' said Peter.

His father's work used to interest him, but now he hated everything to do with it. He hated being a policeman's son, and above all he hated being the son of the head of the Criminal Investigation Department in a small town like Breckham Market, where everyone associated the name Quantrill with the police force. The responsibility was more than he could cope with. He'd had enough of taunts and gibes from his classmates, and of reproaches from adults. What he longed for above all was anonymity.

'Yes,' went on his father, trying hard. After all, the boy was bound to be apprehensive about the coming interview. That made two of them, so the least he could do was to ease the waiting time in as friendly a way as possible. 'It's an interesting case. We don't yet know how the man died, and after this lapse of time we may never know. The significant question is, what happened to his tent and camping gear? The scene-of-crime team have found a few likely items dumped in the bushes, but there's no sign of the bulk of the equipment. If he was murdered, then the murderer might have removed the man's belongings to make it look as though he had packed up and gone. But the fact that the gear isn't there doesn't necessarily point to murder, of course.'

Peter, looking excessively bored, began to whistle through his teeth.

'Did you happen to see anything of a small orange tent in Parson's Close last summer?' his father asked. 'Or did you see or hear anything in the town of an Australian?'

Peter stopped whistling long enough to say, 'Nope.' He was silent for a few minutes and then he said, 'Holy cow. Heowly ceow,' he drawled, in a mock-Australian accent, and then he resumed his whistling.

'Look,' said Douglas Quantrill, making an effort to be patient, 'it's really important for me to find out about this tent. You see, supposing the man died accidentally: we know he was a drinker, and he could have fallen down drunk and died from exposure, or asphyxiation. His tent would then have been left in Parson's Close—but it wouldn't have stayed there indefinitely, would it? Camping equipment costs a packet, you know that.

Someone would sooner or later have noticed that the tent was left unattended, and would have nicked it—don't you agree?'

'If you say so.'

'Oh, for heaven's sake,' snapped Quantrill, showing his irritation at last. 'Use your head, boy—of course it would have been stolen, either bit by bit or in one swoop. And if it was stolen, I need to know. I have to find out what happened to it before I can start to make any sense of the man's death.' He paused, and tried a more conciliatory tone. 'Look, Peter—can you ask around? Some of your mates may know something, or be able to find out something that will help me.'

Peter went very quiet. His face flushed. He pushed himself upright in the armchair. 'Are you asking me—do you expect me—to *inform* on my friends?' he demanded in a tight, angry voice.

'Oh, come on,' Quantrill had protested, trying to cool the situation. '*Inform*'s a ridiculously emotive word. I just want you to help me out—do a bit of detective work for me. You always wanted to do that, didn't you?'

But Peter, choked with indignation and fury, had retorted, 'Get stuffed!'

Then there was the ordeal of listening to the interview between his son and Sergeant Tuckswood. And after that, in bed with Molly, her inevitable post-mortem: how could Peter let them down like this? Where had they, as parents, gone wrong? And what was he, Douglas, proposing to do about the boy in future? Little wonder that he had gone to work next morning in a bad humour.

It was a brighter, milder day. Winter had not yet gone,

but it was visibly in retreat. The sun was low, of course, but it shone through a melting haze for most of the morning, leaving the roads and pavements wet but—except for the gutters—clear for the first time for weeks.

Quantrill sent DC Wigby into the town on a dry tour of the rest of the pubs, with the express purpose of finding out where the Australian had done his drinking; he himself conferred with Inspector Colman, made a press appeal for information about either the Australian or the tent, and meditated, as he drove his car towards St Botolph's Street and the top of Parson's Close, on what young Justin Muttock and Adrian Orris might be concealing.

That the children knew more than they were prepared to say about their acquaintance with Parson's Close, he had no doubt. He hadn't been a father for twenty years without recognizing the glazed look they had assumed when they protested their innocence. He'd seen it in Peter's eyes often enough, blast the boy. And *blast* the boy for his insolence, his surliness, his lack of co-operation, the damage he had helped to cause—

It was at that moment that he saw, trotting ahead of him along the pavement, another boy he knew: Stephen Nash, a year or two younger than Peter, who lived in Benidorm Avenue two doors down from the Quantrills. Stephen, still childish in features and body but with rapidly lengthening legs, was celebrating half-term and sunshine and rising sap by leaping up to grab the lowest branches of the young lime trees that had been planted along the roadside at public expense the previous year. Some of the trees had already died from natural causes; others had been destroyed by just such antics, and Quantrill, a hard-pressed ratepayer at that moment rather than a policeman, was in no mood to dismiss it as youthful high spirits.

He braked abruptly, wrenched open the door, and stood up, one foot on the road. 'Stephen!' he bawled.

Stephen stopped dead in the act of taking off for a jump, chest arched forward, hands up, like one of Robin Hood's outlaws transfixed by the Sheriff of Nottingham's arrow.

'Come here!'

The boy slowly unfroze, turned, and wandered reluctantly towards the Chief Inspector. He gave a nervous, placating grin: 'Hallo, Mr Quantrill.'

'Did you have anything to do with these damaged trees?'

'Me?' said Stephen, his face eloquent of virtue. 'Oh no, Mr Quantrill—I'm not into vandalism now.'

'Kids...' thought Douglas Quantrill sourly, giving him a warning and driving on. During the past twenty-four hours he'd had more than enough of the company of under-eighteens. And it was precisely this disenchantment with youth that induced him to stop the car again in St Botolph's Street and speak to the old man who was hobbling, sly in his slippers, from the Rectory towards the town.

# Chapter 9

Henry Bowers must have been a taller man than Quantrill, in his prime, but age had diminished him. He peered up at the Chief Inspector through the grey furze of his eyebrows.

'I don't know you, do I?' he said almost apprehensively. He glanced along the way he had come, as though afraid that his daughter or her husband would emerge from the Rectory gates and haul him ignominiously back.

And he ought to go back, Quantrill realized that. He must have sneaked out of the house without his daughter's knowledge, because he was inadequately dressed for a February day; he was overcoatless, shivering, and his fabric slippers had already acquired dark toecaps of damp. His breath was harsh in his lungs, his face mottled with cold, his lips purple.

But Quantrill hadn't the heart to take him back to the Rectory immediately. He remembered the old man's frustration over being cooped up in the house during the months of snow, his contempt for the carpeted lounge bar that his son-in-law occasionally took him to, and for the carbonated beer that was served there. What Henry Bowers obviously longed for was a drink in one of the spit-and-sawdust pubs of his young manhood. The spit and sawdust was no longer tolerated, mercifully, but there were still one or two pubs in Breckham Market that hadn't been completely sanitized.

'We met a couple of days ago, when I called at the Rectory,' the Chief Inspector told the old man. 'My name's Quantrill. I was just going for a drink at the Boot. How about joining me?'

He eased Henry Bowers into the car, and out again a couple of hundred yards later. The Boot was one of six pubs in or near the market place. An inn since the eighteenth century, it displayed its sign in the form of a gilt-painted wooden riding-boot that hung from an iron bracket high above the doorway of the narrow flint-faced building. It was smaller than most of the other Breckham pubs, and less easy to convert to modern standards of comfort, and so it had remained essentially a male preserve, a stand-up drinking house.

Quantrill rarely visited the Boot. For one thing, he was unpopular with the landlord; his status was well known to many of the regulars who were inclined to remember, when they saw him, that they had urgent business elsewhere. Besides, he was a staunch Adnams man, and the Boot was a Whitbread house. But it wouldn't hurt to keep old Henry Bowers company for twenty minutes before delivering him back to the Rectory. There was always the chance, Quantrill thought, that he might learn something useful about the Aingers.

'A drop of whiskey, to keep the cold out?' he suggested, parking the old man on a bench between the juke-box and a fruit-machine. It was just after eleven o'clock, and there were no other customers in the bar.

The landlord was civil, but not welcoming. Quantrill bought a half of bitter for himself, and a single Haig. 'Water with it?' he enquired over his shoulder. 'Or ginger?'

Henry Bowers shook his head. Saliva was beginning

to dribble from one corner of his mouth, and his eyes were glittering in anticipation. 'Don't spoil it,' he croaked, reaching out a great gnarled hand to envelop the glass. Quantrill, suddenly conscientious, hoped that there was no good medical reason for what seemed to have been a lengthy abstention from spirits.

'Bes' respects,' muttered the old man, raising his glass. He took a gulp, wiped his mouth with the back of his hand, and let out a long quavering sigh. 'What did you say your name was?' he asked presently.

'Doug Quantrill. I came to the Rectory the other day to see your daughter.'

Henry Bowers nodded, and sat brooding for a moment. 'She's a good girl to me, our Gilly. Don't think I don't know that. I should be in a mess without her, now that her dear mother's gone.' The facile tears of age gathered in his eyes. He raised his glass and drained it. 'That was my second wife, y'know. Nearly twenty year younger than me—you'd ha' thought she ha' lasted better, wouldn't you? I reckoned I'd picked a good strong 'un, second time round. Thought to meself, Well, she'll see you out, Henry me boy. You'll be all right now, she'll take care o' you in your old age. And now look what I've come to...' He stared down at his damp slippers that were steaming in the heat from the gas fire. A dewdrop began to accumulate at the bulbous tip of his nose.

'But you've got Gillian,' Quantrill reminded him when he had fetched another whiskey. 'You're lucky there.'

'Ar, I am lucky. She's the only one I ever had, out of two marriages, and she's a good 'un. But she never should ha' married *him*.' He spoke the pronoun so viciously that the dewdrop wobbled off and plopped on to the lapel of his jacket.

'A suitable marriage, I should have thought,' said Quantrill.

'*Suitable!*' Henry Bowers hawked so contemptuously that Quantrill instinctively moved his feet in case a spit followed, but the old man swallowed whiskey instead. 'No...' he brooded. 'For all his father was a parson and his granddad was a rural dean, and I never had mor'n twenty acres and a few dairy cows, I don't mind telling you that our Gillian married beneath her. She's got more brains in her little finger than he's got in his big head.

'I'd say nothing if she'd had children, mind. A young woman ought to raise a family. Well, it don't always happen, I know that, and not for want of trying. But if she can't have a family, she ought to be putting her brains to use. A doctor, that's what she set her heart on being when she was at school, and I'd have supported her all the way. I've worked hard all me life, and saved every penny I could, and I shouldn't ha' cared what it cost me. I think the world of our Gilly, I'd do anything for her. But no, she had to go and marry this Robin when she was only nineteen, and she's played second fiddle to him ever since. It's Robin this and Robin that, everything has to revolve round bloody Robin.'

'Perhaps she's happy like that.'

'Hah! And p'r'aps *I'm* happy like *this*. He's got a lot to answer for, that Robin Ainger. How he's got the nerve to stand up in the pulpit telling folks to be Christians, I don't know. There's things I could tell you—what did you say your name was?'

'Just call me Doug.'

But the old man evidently thought that he had already said too much about his daughter and her husband. 'Nice drop o' whiskey,' he said, raising his glass. 'Bes' respects, Doug.'

'Another?'

Henry Bowers cackled with sly amusement. 'Hadn't better—might get into trouble.'

Quantrill pushed it as hard as he dared: 'You'd be welcome.'

'No—it wouldn't do, would it? Mustn't let the Rector down, must I? That's why they try not to let me out on me own, y'know...mustn't talk about Robin. Got a position in the town to keep up.'

'That's true,' agreed the Chief Inspector, sorry that he was to hear no more but relieved that his offer had been refused; he didn't want to be accused of getting the Rector's father-in-law drunk. 'Tell me something, though, Henry; do you remember a young Australian who came to Breckham last summer? He used to camp in Parson's Close.'

'Oh ar,' said Henry Bowers, uninterested. He picked at a crevice in his discoloured teeth with a horny finger-nail and concentrated his attention on the men who were beginning to drift into the pub, each with a newspaper folded open at the racing page and a pencil at the ready. The weather had disrupted the racing calendar, and Breckham's middle-aged punters were anxious for action now that the snow had cleared from some of the courses. The Boot was next door to the betting-shop, and as usual they had called in to study the odds over a quiet pint while they waited for the shop to open.

'Did you happen to see the Australian?' Quantrill persisted.

'Might've done.' The old man cackled again. 'Bloody Aussies,' he said, but this time he used the adjective without malice. 'I fought along o' them in the first world war, at Gallipoli, y'know. Talk about swearing, I never heard such language afore or since. Good fighters, though, the

Aussies. Not that there was any hope of winning, what with the heat and hardly any drinking water, and the ground littered with stinking corpses, and the flies and dysentery—but we did our bit.'

There was nothing to be gained from listening to the old man's reminiscences, so Quantrill finished his beer and stood up. 'Come on, Henry. Better get you back home before your daughter sends out a search party.'

The old man squinted up at him. 'I ha' killed a few men, in me time, y'know,' he said.

'I daresay you have. My old Dad used to tell me the same—he was in your war, and he reckoned he put paid to a few Jerries.'

'Not Jerries,' said Henry Bowers impatiently. 'Turcos!' His faded eyes focused on the distant past. 'They were up in the hills above Suvla Plain, pinning us down. We were ordered to advance across the plain on August the 12th, in broad daylight. There was only rocks and scrub for cover, and our bayonets shone in the sun and gave us away. The Turcos picked us off like rabbits. But then the scrub caught fire, and the smoke covered our advance. We took 'em by surprise, and I got two or three on 'em before we had to withdraw. There were only a few of us left by then, o' course. That's when I were wounded—'

'You must tell me about it sometime.' Quantrill levered the old man up from the bench, led him outside, fitted him into the car, and drove to the Rectory. 'Drop you at the gate, shall I?'

'That'll do well. Our Gilly's gone to Yarchester and *he's* messing about in the church. They'll never know I've been out.'

'They will if they smell your breath,' said Quantrill, extricating him from the car and steering him through the gate.

Henry Bowers gave him a slow, grotesque, conspiratorial wink. 'I ha' got some peppermints in me room. Thank y' kindly for the drink—what did you say your name was, again?'

The Aingers were bound to get to know that he had talked to the old man; better come clean. 'If your family ask, tell them you were with Chief Inspector Quantrill. You can say that it was my idea to go to the pub—you were in police custody.'

As he drove off he glanced back and saw Henry Bowers standing where he had left him, slack knee'd, open-mouthed, looking as though having a drink on a policeman was astonishing enough to bring the world to an end.

Quantrill had originally intended to take another look at Parson's Close, but now he changed his mind and went in search of Robin Ainger. He found him in the church porch, pinning up on the noticeboard a list of services for the coming week.

He greeted him. 'I've just been talking to your father-in-law,' he added.

The Rector bent to retrieve a fallen drawing-pin. 'Oh yes—you've been to the Rectory?'

'No. I happened to see him pottering along St Botolph's Street, going towards the town in his slippers. He told me the other day that he was longing to go out, so I'm afraid I took it upon myself to suggest that he came with me for a drink at the Boot.'

Robin Ainger's handsome jaw tightened. For a moment he said nothing, but then he gave Quantrill a tepid smile. 'That was very kind of you. I try to give him an occasional change of scenery, but I think what he appreciates most is a new audience for his stories. His conversation is inevitably limited—as you discovered, no doubt?'

'Gallipoli, mostly,' said Quantrill.

'Ah yes—Suvla Plain: heat, flies, dysentery, and what he calls Turcos. August 1915's a lot clearer to him than the week before last. He's old enough to be Gillian's grandfather, of course. His first wife died young, and he married again in his fifties—but I expect he told you more than you wanted to know about the family?'

'He did say that he knows how lucky he is to have a good daughter, and to be looked after in his old age. What he really wanted to talk about was Gallipoli, but his slippers were damp so I returned him to the Rectory as soon as I decently could. None of my business, Mr Ainger, but now that the snow's gone it'd be as well if he wore his shoes. He's obviously a stubborn old boy, and determined to go out whether he's suitably dressed or not.'

The Rector's jaw tightened again, and he busied himself with the noticeboard. 'I'm sure you're right,' he murmured, courteous but stiff with resentment.

'As I said,' Quantrill apologized quickly, 'it's none of my business. It's all very well for outsiders to be patient and sympathetic with old people for ten minutes at a time, isn't it? I do realize that it's much tougher for those who have to live with them and look after them.'

'Yes,' said Robin Ainger. He jammed in a final drawing pin, screwing it down hard with his thumb, and then excused himself to talk to the verger.

Edgar Blore, the dignity of his cassock marred by the collar of his fawn cardigan which protruded unevenly from the neckband, was fidgeting urgently in the doorway of the church. The Rector joined him for a conference about a delivery of heating-oil that had failed to arrive, and Quantrill studied the noticeboard while he waited.

The congregation of St Botolph's was evidently kept busy, with fund-raising activities for the restoration of the angel roof and rehearsals for an Easter performance of Handel's *Messiah*. Rotas detailed the female members for cleaning the church silver, providing and arranging flowers, and serving coffee in the church hall after the 10.30 family service on Sunday mornings.

Visitors were not neglected either. Various notices exhorted them not to leave the church without a prayer, to contribute to the restoration fund, to Shut the Door Please, and to Mind the Steps. They were also advised, in thick black fibrepoint on a large sheet of paper pinned in the most prominent position, that *Rubbings may be taken of the monumental brasses* ONLY BY APPOINTMENT. WRITTEN PERMISSION MUST *be obtained from the* RECTOR *to whom the appropriate* FEE *towards church expenses* MUST *be paid.*

'Have you any more information,' said Robin Ainger, turning back to the Chief Inspector, 'about the body in the Close?'

'Not yet.' Quantrill repeated to him what he had told his son about the disappearance of the camping gear. 'Have you any notion what might have happened to the tent, Mr Ainger?'

'I'm afraid not. But I'd go along with your reasoning, certainly. If the body is Athol's, and if his tent was left erected, then it's likely that someone would have taken it. After all, although it couldn't be seen from St Botolph Street, it must have been in full view of the by-pass. Whoever took it probably had no connection at all with Breckham Market.'

'But it just might have been someone local. You don't

happen to know of any youngster who suddenly acquired a tent last summer, I suppose? He wouldn't necessarily have stolen it, but he might have been tempted to buy it dirt cheap.'

'I haven't heard of anything like that.' Robin Ainger picked up the duffle coat that he had left bundled on the stone bench in the porch, and began to put it on. 'Incidentally—I've been meaning to ask you this ever since we first found the body—what will happen to the remains? Assuming that they are Athol Garrity's.'

'If they're his, it'll be a matter for the Australian authorities to arrange with his family. There don't seem to have been any enquiries about him, so the family can't be too anxious; even so, they might want what's left of him flown back for burial. If he's to stay here, the coroner's officer will have to fix something up as soon as the remains are released. The costs will have to be met from local funds, and you'll probably find yourself called in to officiate.'

'That's what I thought. And what I wanted to say is that if the burial is to be here, I shall be glad to officiate. After all, I knew him slightly. I feel that it's the least I can do for his family.'

Quantrill gave the Rector a straight and narrow look. 'I'm sure they'd appreciate it,' he said. 'They'll be glad to know that he died among friends.'

Robin Ainger muttered something about telephoning the oil company and turned away abruptly, red to the roots of his wavy hair.

# Chapter 10

The Rector hurried off, between ranks of simple eighteenth-century gravestones that leaned towards each other as though the cherubs whose heads and wings appeared in relief at the top of each stone were harmonizing in perpetuity. The Chief Inspector was about to follow when it occurred to him that he had never, in his ten years at Breckham Market, entered the church, except dutifully and reluctantly for an occasional wedding or funeral. This might be a good opportunity to look round, and at the same time talk to the verger. He pushed open the massive oak door, with its elaborate horizontal fleur-de-lys iron hinges, and stepped down into the fifteenth century.

He expected to encounter the smell of the dark interior of the older, smaller church in the Suffolk village where he had been brought up, a compound of dank stone and mouldering hassocks that he had assumed to be the essence of Anglicanism. But in St Botolph's, this smell was completely absent. The church was not exactly warm, but the chill had been taken off it. It was lofty and remarkably light.

The parish church of Breckham Market had had the great good fortune to escape the over-zealous attentions of Victorian restorers, and so most of the woodwork was original. The low benches were silver-grey oak, their arms carved into figures worn so smooth by the handling of generations of worshippers that it was difficult to decide whether the subjects were sacred or secular. What could be discerned of the figures' short tunics and pudding-basin haircuts suggested that the carving had been done some time between Agincourt and the Wars of the Roses.

There was an unfortunate east window in the chancel, commemorating a late nineteenth-century Rector in glass that was stained a bilious art-nouveau yellow; otherwise, apart from some fifteenth-century fragments in the north aisle, the glass was completely plain. Light, all the brighter for being reflected from the untouched snow that lingered in the churchyard, flooded in not only from the windows in the aisles but also from the high windows of the clerestory.

The height of the nave was impressive. Quantrill's eye instinctively followed the line of the stone pillars up towards the wooden roof, every detail of which was clearly illuminated. The roof was supported by an alternation of tie and hammer beams, and from the ends of the hammer beams great wooden angels stretched their wings and floated face to face across the void.

'What you might call uplifting, don't you think, Mr Quantrill?'

The Chief Inspector had never, to his knowledge, met the verger; but he had become accustomed to being known by sight and reputation to far more people than he himself knew. The local newspaper had a photograph of him on file, and reproduced it to help fill their columns whenever he was working on a serious crime and was unable to give them any hard news about it. But although he had never heard of Edgar Blore before that week, Quantrill had now seen him mentioned twice in reports from DC Wigby: once in his capacity as caretaker of the vandalized church hall, and again when he had told Wigby about the Australian girl who had visited the Rectory. The verger, he calculated, was likely to know as much as anyone in Breckham Market about the Reverend Robin Ainger.

'A very fine roof, Mr Blore,' Quantrill agreed. 'I expect you have a lot of visitors here in the summer?'

'Oh yes, from all over the world. And not just because of the roof. The monumental brasses are our real glory, of course.'

'So I believe. I must have a look at them while I'm here.'

The verger drew a deep breath, twitched anxiously at his moustache, and began a rambling, mournful apology for having named the Chief Inspector's son as one of the likely church hall culprits. Quantrill interrupted to reassure him that he had done the right thing, and then steered the conversation back to the church brasses. He knew nothing about brass-rubbing, but Ainger had said that Athol Garrity had professed an interest in it; and judging by the notice in the porch, brass-rubbers gave the Rector a considerable amount of harassment.

Having stopped twitching, the verger rolled back some drab strips of carpet to reveal eight figures engraved on brass, set into slabs in the worn stone floor of the church. Four of the figures were at the east end of the south aisle, two at the foot of the chancel steps and two more, the finest, in the chancel itself, close to the altar rail. Some were almost life-sized, some no more than twelve inches long. All of them had been placed with their feet towards the altar, so that, when the bodies in the graves beneath rose up on resurrection day, they would come face to face with God.

The clarity of detail, five centuries on, was astonishing. Here, with every joint in the men's plate armour, every fold in the women's gowns, every elaboration in their headdress, clearly visible, were the leading citizens of fifteenth-century Breckham Market. Having stared for several minutes, intrigued, at the largest knight's long hooked nose, cleft chin and drooping moustaches, the Chief Inspector felt—even though the brass might have been a medieval form of identikit rather than a definitive portrait—that he would have a good chance of recognizing Sir John Bedingfield if he were ever to meet him.

There were Bedingfields in and around Breckham Market still, though they looked nothing like Sir John. They were a swarthy, shiftless, pugnacious tribe, so frequently in trouble that whenever a petty crime was committed the police checked them out first. Sir John and the high-nosed lady at his side would have disowned them on sight, thought Quantrill, amused.

'They're very fine brasses, Mr Blore,' he said. 'Very interesting. No wonder you get a lot of visitors to the church. An Australian was here last summer, the Rector told me.'

'Would that be the man Mr Wigby was asking me about?'

'That's right—we think that the skeleton in Parson's Close might be his. But DC Wigby didn't know, when he spoke to you, that the Australian had been inside the church. Mr Ainger tells me that he was interested in the brasses, and that he camped in the meadow while he was making some rubbings. Are you sure you don't recollect him?'

'Quite sure. I'm sorry I can't help you, Mr Quantrill, but we're over-run every summer with strangers who come to rub the brasses, and I try not to get involved with them. It's my ulcer, you see. Oh, most of them are not much trouble. They bring a big sheet of white paper and spread it out on a brass and spend hours crouched over it, rubbing away with a stick of heelball to get the impression of the figure on the paper. They're quiet and neat and tidy, and I make no complaint about them at all. But others...'

The verger began to work himself up into a state of high moral indignation: 'You wouldn't credit what some of them do, Mr Quantrill. I could hardly contain myself over their behaviour when I first became verger—and of course it made my ulcer play up. In the end, Mr Ainger told me to let him deal with the brass-rubbers. He keeps the appointments book now, and sorts out all the problems.'

'I saw the notice in the porch,' said Quantrill. 'I gather that some of the rubbers don't make appointments, and try to get out of paying the fees.'

'That's not the half of it!' Edgar Blore spluttered. 'It's behaviour I'm talking about, and reverence. Appointments are important, you see, because most of the rubbers aren't churchgoers and so they don't take the services into consideration. Many's the time—before Mr Ainger began the appointments system—that I've come to prepare the church for a service and found that I couldn't get into the chancel without tripping over somebody. And when I asked them to move, some of them were really belligerent. And then they'd argue when I asked them to pay! It's not that we charge much, but it's the principle of the thing. Don't you agree, Mr Quantrill?'

The Chief Inspector made assenting noises, and bent to help the verger roll the carpets back over the brasses to protect them from wear.

'After all,' continued Edgar Blore, neatly straightening one of the carpets that Quantrill had replaced, 'the expense of maintaining the fabric of a church like this is alarming. To my mind anyone who visits it, let alone makes use of it, should expect to make a contribution towards its upkeep. And then, it isn't as if every rubber is doing it out of historical interest. Some of them make it into a commercial enterprise. Why, you can see rubbings of these very brasses in art and craft shops in Yarchester. People pay pounds, especially if the rubbers have used gold heelball on black paper, to have them as wall-hangings. It's a racket, that's what it is. And if I told you the way some of the rubbers behave when they're here in church—even when they've made an appointment and paid a fee—you wouldn't believe me.'

After twenty-five years in the force, Douglas Quantrill found nothing in human nature incredible. He had no difficulty at all in believing that a small minority of people could be greedy, abusive, pigheaded and bloody-minded, in church as well as out of it. What interested him in the conversation was the glimpse the verger had given of some of the unexpected stresses that went with the Rector's job. Until that week, Quantrill had unthinkingly assumed that being a parson was a soft option. During the past few days he had begun to learn that this was far from being true.

'Tell me about it, Mr Blore?' he suggested.

The verger, having adjusted the carpets to his satisfaction, brushed down his cassock with the flat of his hand. 'As I say, it's a question of reverence. Some of the rubbers seem to have no idea that this is a place of worship. Instead of bringing masking-tape to hold down the paper while they're rubbing on it, they use piles of prayer books—even the big Bible from the lectern. They have picnics in the choir stalls, and drop litter on the floor. And sometimes they bring small children and let them run wild, dressing up in the choir surplices, racing round the aisles, meddling with the bell ropes—'

He paused for breath, trembling with indignation. 'And one day last year—you'll never credit this, Mr Quantrill—one day early last summer I came in by the south door and heard a terrible racket going on. And there was a young man, with a transistor radio going full blast, sitting on the altar swinging his legs and drinking out of a can!'

Even Quantrill was startled. '*Sitting* on the altar?'

'*Sitting* on the *altar.* I told you that you wouldn't credit it! I was so furious that I couldn't bring myself to speak to him. I rushed straight round to the church hall and telephoned the Rector. He came roaring down St Botolph's Street in his car at sixty miles an hour and strode into the church like—' the verger lifted his eyes for inspiration and found it in the magnificent timbers of the roof '—like an avenging angel. I wouldn't have cared to be in *that* young man's shoes!'

'What happened?'

Edgar Blore shook his head. 'I didn't come back to find out. Mr Ainger told me to stay in the church hall and make myself a cup of tea, so I did.' His sad eyes looked defensively at the Chief Inspector. 'I suppose you think it was cowardly of me, but the Rector understands about my ulcer. Besides, he's younger and bigger than I am.'

'Yes, of course. Though it does seem to me,' added Quantrill, 'that he hasn't looked so well lately. He seems to have lost a lot of his drive.'

The verger had begun to move down the south aisle towards the door, and for a moment Quantrill thought that he was too loyal to the Rector to want to discuss him. But Edgar Blore was merely choosing his words, and when he spoke it was with some relief.

'To tell you the truth—and I haven't said this to anyone else, except Mrs Blore—that's what I've felt. The Rector hasn't been his old self for months now. I'm beginning to think that he's lost heart, and that's a sad condition for a parson. But then, he has a lot to contend with—as you and I know, Mr Quantrill.'

The verger gave the Chief Inspector a meaningful nod, and did not elaborate.

'Mr Ainger's very well thought of in the town,' commented Quantrill.

'Indeed he is! A very popular Rector. I put it down to the fact that he's not trendy. Trendiness doesn't do in a parish like Breckham Market. Mr Ainger's only a young man, but I'm glad to say that he believes in upholding all the old standards.'

'Quite right,' agreed Quantrill. They had reached the south door and he put out his hand to the massive iron latch. 'Well, I'm glad to have had the opportunity of—'

The verger stood quite still and gave a discreet but firm cough behind his clenched fist. His eyes moved from the Chief Inspector's to the padlocked box that was fixed to the wall just inside the door. On the box was pinned a handwritten label: *Church Expenses*.

Shamed into giving, Quantrill scrabbled in his trouser pocket and emerged with a palmful of small bronze coins and a solitary ten-pence piece. He looked at them doubtfully, raised an eyebrow at the verger, saw the reproach in his gaze, took out his wallet and pushed a folded pound note into the box.

'By the way, Mr Blore,' he said, deciding to put the money down against expenses and to extract as much information as possible on the strength of it, 'that badly behaved brass-rubber you told me about—the young man you saw sitting on the altar: did you hear his voice? I'm wondering whether it could have been the Australian we're interested in.'

The verger twitched his moustache in thought, then shook his head. 'No, I'm sorry. I couldn't face speaking to him myself, you see—I left it to the Rector, so I never heard the man's voice. You'll have to ask Mr Ainger. He's the one who can tell you.'

Quantrill didn't doubt it. But whether the Reverend Robin Ainger *would* tell him was, he knew, a different matter.

# Chapter 11

'County operations room, Inspector Tait here.'

'Quantrill, Breckham Market. Can we have a word?'

'One moment.'

The Chief Inspector grinned to himself as he sat at his desk with the telephone receiver at his ear. There were times, he knew, when the operations room at county police headquarters could seem as busy as the control tower at Heathrow; but had there been a major incident in progress, the switchboard would not have put him through. Young Martin Tait, formerly his sergeant, was simply playing a power game.

'...and let me know as soon as it comes up on the VDU,' he heard the new Inspector say in his clipped, efficient voice. Then, 'Good to hear from you, sir. How can I help?'

'I thought it was high time we met for a drink. You know how it is at Breckham—we're so busy hoeing our sugar-beet fields that we lose sight of the outside world. I'd be interested to hear what the view's like from county HQ.'

'Oh.' Tait sounded disappointed, as though he had hoped that the Chief Inspector had a more significant motive for calling him. 'I'd certainly like to meet, but life's very busy at the moment.'

'I was afraid of that. Pity. I'd hoped we could arrange something between now and Friday—but if you're too busy it doesn't matter.'

'What's special about Friday?'

'A coroner's inquest... Well, never mind. We can have that drink some other time.'

'Is that the resumed inquest on the Parson's Close skeleton? Look, I really would like to see you again, sir. I'm off duty tomorrow afternoon, and as it happens I'll be coming into your division. Could you meet me at the old airfield at Horkey—say half-past two?'

'At Horkey? What in thunder are you going there for?'

'I belong to the aero club that operates from there. I'm learning to fly.'

'Good grief,' said Quantrill, conceding the round. 'Well, yes. See you tomorrow then.'

'Hang on! What about that skeleton? Was forensic able to establish the cause of death?'

'No. So it looks as though it'll be an open verdict, and the file will be closed. But I'm not at all happy about it.'

'And you'd like my help?'

'Let's say that I thought it might be an idea if we were to talk it over.'

Inspector Tait's sigh of satisfaction came clearly along the line. 'I began to think you'd never ask,' he said.

A little orange and white two-seater Cessna 152 aircraft, its cockpit considerably smaller than the front seats of a Mini, stood outside the premises of the Horkey aero club, rocking against its brakes in the March wind. One of its hangar companions had just taken off from the grass airfield, lurching drunkenly into the air under the control of a student pilot. Quantrill couldn't bear to look. It was just possible to believe that the frail contraption would get off the ground in one piece, but considerably more difficult to feel confident about the landing.

'You'll never get *me* up in one of those things,' he declared.

Martin Tait laughed indulgently. 'That was what the caterpillar said about the butterfly. You really can't stay earthbound all your life. Come on, admit it, you're longing to go up.'

'No, I'm not,' said Quantrill, holding on to his hat, 'and certainly not in a little tin can like that.' He had never yet had occasion to travel by air, and although he had not entirely lost his boyhood longing to go up in an aeroplane he intended his first experience to be in something more substantial. 'Anyway, you couldn't take me up. You haven't got your private pilot's licence yet.'

'That won't take long,' said Tait confidently. 'I've already done twenty hours' dual flying, and four solo. Another ten hours' dual and six solo, and that's it.'

'That's all?'

'Oh, there are exams to pass too. But forty hours is the minimum flying-time for a student pilot before qualification.'

'And you think it won't take you more than the minimum?'

'I shall be ashamed of myself if it does. Come and have a drink, we've got a club licence.'

Quantrill followed the former detective, a slight, sharp, fair young man, dapper in a good leather jacket and a rollneck sweater, into the renovated wartime hut that served as a clubroom. He accepted a can of lager; Tait, who was due for a flying lesson in an hour's time, confined himself to machine-made coffee. The aero-club staff were in the control tower, and the two policemen had the slightly battered club lounge to themselves.

'How are things at HQ?' asked Quantrill.

'Interesting. Really interesting. I enjoy having so much technology at my disposal—computer terminal, visual display units, radio, telex, teleprinter, direct lines to all the neighbouring forces' control rooms, and to New Scotland Yard and Interpol... I can find out anything I want to know within a few minutes.'

'Simpler than plodding round Breckham trying to dig out information at grass-roots level,' reflected Quantrill. 'It took Yarchester less time to get confirmation that the skeleton in Parson's Close was Athol James Garrity, aged twenty-four, late of Queensland, Australia, than it did for Ian Wigby to track down which Breckham pub the man used. All the same, neither technology nor forensic science has been able to tell us how he met his death.'

'What do we know about him?'

Quantrill passed on the information that he and Wigby had pieced together, adding, 'It seemed at first that no one in the town had met him, apart from the Aingers. But then we found that he'd done his drinking in the Concorde, one of the pubs on the new estate. He could easily walk there from Parson's Close, across the by-pass. They remember him quite well at the Concorde—he drank a lot and was noisy, but never argumentative or belligerent. He certainly didn't make any enemies. He had several casual drinking companions, but he always came and went on his own.

'He last went there on the evening of July 29th. The barman remembers the date because it was his first day back after his summer holiday. Garrity was at the Concorde at six o'clock, waiting for it to open. He'd been away too, he said, staying with Australian friends in London. He'd just hitched a lift back, the weather was warm, and he was thirsty. He downed four or five pints, possibly more, and by eight o'clock when the barmaid came on duty he was cross-eyed. Soon afterwards he mumbled something about going back to his tent for a kip, and staggered off. No one from the Concorde saw him after that.'

'But someone might have seen him crossing the by-pass,' said Tait quickly. 'If he was staggering drunk, he'd have been noticeable. Have you thought that he might have been struck by a hit-and-run driver, and then managed to crawl as far as the bushes before collapsing? Have you considered—?'

'Yes,' snapped Quantrill, who had temporarily forgotten Tait's unfailing ability to get right up his nose. 'We've done a thorough job—if you'll just wait until I've finished. Garrity was in fact seen again, later that same evening. The Rector and his wife say that they saw him by chance from the Rectory garden, at about half-past nine. They were standing in the drive, and they saw him weaving along St Botolph Street from the direction of the town, heading for the gate at the top of Parson's Close. That means that after he left the Concorde he must have gone up into the town—but that's where we've drawn a blank. We haven't been able to discover where he went or what he did.'

Inspector Tait's expression made it clear that had he still been CID Sergeant at Breckham Market, the investigation would have been more productive.

'Didn't you discover that the Aingers had an Australian girl visitor last summer?' he said. 'I met her one evening when I went there for coffee. They mentioned someone called Athol, and I gathered that he was making a nuisance of himself by hanging round the girl. He probably went to see her after he left the Concorde.'

Quantrill stared at Tait irritably. 'Yes, of course we found out about Janey Rolph. I'd very much like to talk to her, but she's left the country. The Aingers say that she was with them for the whole of that evening—but the question is, are they telling the truth? So what's all this about your going there for coffee? Ainger told me that he knew you, but I assumed it was in your official capacity. Why the hell didn't you say sooner that you knew them socially? They're the biggest puzzle in this enquiry.'

'And how was I supposed to know that? Anyway, I assumed that you knew them as well as I did. It's part of the job, as I see it, to establish a good relationship with the leaders of the community. If you'd told me that the Aingers were puzzling you, I'd have come over to help as soon as you started the enquiry.'

It would be a waste of time to take umbrage. Quantrill helped himself to another can of lager at Tait's expense instead, and told him his grounds for suspicion. 'I've now talked to them, together or separately, at least five times,' he concluded, 'and understandably they're getting restive. They've volunteered a certain amount of information, but I'm inclined to think that they're simply trying to cover themselves by anticipating what we might find out from other sources. They now insist that they know nothing more than they've already told me. I think that's a lie, but there's damn all I can do about it. When a man's a parson, it's hard to suggest to him that he's not telling the whole truth.'

'The real trouble,' said Tait, going straight to the point, 'is that forensic hasn't been able to establish whether or not a crime has been committed. If this was a murder enquiry you could pull Robin Ainger in, parson or not, and persuade him to talk.'

'Him or her. I'm certain they're in this together—not necessarily concealing a crime, but concealing *something* from us. They're both under considerable stress at the moment—though that's partly accounted for by Gillian's father. He's infirm, and becoming childish.'

'The old man must have deteriorated a lot since last summer, then,' said Tait. 'He was lively enough when I saw him, and working in the garden.'

'He's had back trouble, so his daughter said, and the bad weather didn't help him. He knows, or suspects, something too—though he dislikes his son-in-law, so perhaps he's just being malicious. Anyway, he's being cussed with his daughter, and she's nearly at the end of her tether. But even if we make allowances for their domestic problems, and for the strain of their job, it doesn't account for the way they're behaving. You know them better than I do, Martin; what was your impression of them?'

Tait shied his empty coffee beaker into a waste-bin. The aero club was chronically short of funds, and members were expected to clear away their own empties.

'The Aingers have been under considerable stress for months,' he said. 'Marital problems. They were hospitable enough, but it seemed a desperate kind of hospitality. I felt that they were beginning to grab at people in order to avoid being alone with each other. It was an interesting situation to observe, but it didn't make for a comfortable evening out. The tension between them was hardly disguised on my last visit.'

'When was that?'

'The last week in June, just before I started my summer leave. I kept out of their way after I came back. I'd promised Robin that I'd talk to the youth club in September about CID work, but I never went back to the Rectory. I wouldn't have been at all surprised to hear that their marriage had broken up by now.'

'A parson can't very well admit to that kind of human frailty,' said Quantrill. 'A divorce would put an end to his career. Even a separation would ruin his credibility—after all, if he can't keep his marriage going, what hope is there for the rest of us? But from what I've seen in the past few weeks, the Aingers' partnership seems to be working reasonably well now. What did you think was their trouble?'

'He bullied her, and she let him. That must have been what drew them together in the first place,' said Tait, an observant bachelor who liked to think himself something of an expert on marriage. 'I don't know what had happened to intensify their difficulties, but it seemed that when anyone or anything in the parish upset Robin, he'd come home and direct his anger at Gillian. She spent her time trying to placate him, offering herself as a doormat in an attempt to keep him happy. She even encouraged him to talk to the Australian girl because he so obviously liked her. Anyone could see what a fool thing that was for her to do, but I suppose she imagined that because her husband was a parson—'

Tait bit off his sentence and shot to his feet, his eyes bright, his nose sharp. 'God, what a potentially explosive situation! The Aingers' marriage was fraying under tension, and then along came Janey Rolph with Athol Garrity somewhere in tow... And the point is that Janey was stunning, absolutely stunning—small and delicate, with pale skin, big brown eyes, and the most fantastic hair I've ever seen: a thick, vivid red, cut quite short all over so that it looked like a fox's pelt. I didn't see her for more than fifteen minutes—and on my last visit before going on leave, otherwise I'd have been after her myself—but I shan't forget her in a hurry. They had another visitor at the time, and he couldn't take his eyes off her either. More significantly, nor could Robin Ainger.'

Quantrill sat up. When Gillian Ainger had told him about the post-graduate student she had befriended, he had imagined someone earnest, shy, myopic. It hadn't occurred to him that a man as good-looking as Ainger would have been interested in the girl.

'How did Janey Rolph react to him?'

Tait stood taut, thinking hard. 'My impression was that she behaved very tactfully. She was obviously accustomed to admiration, and knew how to deal with it. I remember thinking that she was giving quite as much attention to Gillian as she did to Ainger. She seemed to be encouraging them to communicate with each other doing her best to bring them back together.'

'Mrs Ainger didn't resent her, then?'

'Not in the least. She obviously liked the girl, and assumed that her husband was bomb-proof, though anyone could see that Janey had knocked him sideways. But the fact that he, as a parson, couldn't do anything about Janey would make the situation infinitely worse for him.'

'Good God ...' Quantrill pushed himself up out of his armchair and began to pace the clubroom, awed by the hypothesis. 'And Garrity was following Janey about... She didn't like him, according to Mrs Ainger, but that wouldn't stop Ainger feeling jealous. He disliked Garrity anyway, he told me that—'

'And Ainger is a tall man,' contributed Tait, 'and he has a temper. I've seen him go white with rage—'

Quantrill took a sobering breath. 'We haven't a scrap of evidence to indicate how Garrity met his death,' he remembered.

'No. But between us, we know enough to confront the Aingers. Garrity's death might well have been an accident, but from what you've told me it sounds as though the Aingers know something about it. If we make the right approach we ought to be able to get an admission from one or other of them. We could—'

'"We"?' interrupted the Chief Inspector in charge of Breckham Market divisional CID.

The HQ Inspector (Ops) was crestfallen. 'Ah, hell, for a moment I'd forgotten my promotion. Look, sir, technology's all very well, but I miss CID work. Let me in on your interview with the Aingers, please. I know it'd be irregular, but after all it's my information you're working on.'

'Which is exactly why I've no intention of having you with me,' said Quantrill firmly. 'Not that I'm ungrateful, but it may turn out that the Aingers have perfectly clear consciences, and I've got to go on living in the town with them. I don't want to be accused of encouraging you to abuse their hospitality by telling me about their private lives.'

Tait shrugged. 'Let me know how it goes, then,' he said distantly. He looked at his watch. 'I'm due for my pre-flight briefing in ten minutes, but I'll walk back with you to your car.'

The two men left the club hut and walked towards the parked cars, along an asphalted perimeter track scoured dry as a bone by March winds. 'How's the family?' asked Tait politely.

'Perfectly well in health, thanks. You've heard about Peter's misdeeds, though, I suppose?'

'We do get to hear most things at county HQ.'

'Bloody fine state of affairs,' grumbled Quantrill, 'when a Chief Inspector's son appears before a juvenile court accused of malicious damage. He said that the trouble in the church hall started as horseplay, and admitted taking part in it. All the youngsters involved say that the worst of the damage was done by a raiding-party—whether they're telling the truth God knows. I certainly don't. Anyway, Peter was conditionally discharged, with a fine that'll take all his pocket money for the next six months. What he'll get up to while he's broke I dread to—'

'And how's Alison?' interrupted Tait abruptly.

Quantrill glanced sideways at his colleague, who had last year taken an unexpectedly serious liking to his younger daughter. 'She rings us from London every week, and sounds very cheerful,' he said.

'Has she got herself engaged yet?'

'No, no. She mentions various names, but there doesn't seem to be anyone special. She's only twenty, there's plenty of time before she thinks about settling down.'

'Tell her I asked after her,' said Tait. 'And thanks for coming over, sir.'

'Thanks a lot for your help, Martin.' Quantrill turned his head to watch, fascinated despite himself, as one of the little aircraft rose gracefully—presumably in the hands of a qualified pilot—into the limitless cool blue of the sky.

'How much is this flying game costing you?' he demanded.

'It'll be roughly a thousand to qualify, with club and exam fees and everything,' said Tait matter-of-factly.

'A *thousand pounds?*' Quantrill's eyes bulged as he thought what he could do with that kind of spare money, if he had it. 'You'd better stay a bachelor if you want to indulge in this as a hobby. Rather you than me, anyway. I prefer to keep my feet on the ground and make the most of married bliss.'

Tait, who knew that the course of Quantrill's marriage had been less than blissful, gave his former chief a grin. 'Envious?' he asked.

'Not on your life.' Quantrill craned his neck to watch the aircraft, now small as a butterfly, catching sunlight on its wings as it forged confidently upwards. For a moment he tried to imagine himself in Tait's position: young, unencumbered, assured of accelerated promotion, affluent, free as air. Then, 'Oh, all right, of course I am,' he admitted ruefully. 'Envious as hell, boy, envious as hell.'

# Chapter 12

The following morning at ten o'clock the Reverend Robin and Mrs Ainger presented themselves, as urgently requested by the Chief Inspector, at Breckham Market police station. Quantrill was waiting for them in his office. They entered subdued, stiff with apprehension. He greeted them with a straight face and offered them neither coffee nor small talk.

'I wanted to have a few words with you about the progress of our enquiry into the death of Athol James Garrity,' he began.

They sat silent, stiff as a pair of hypnotized rabbits, watching the words come out of his mouth.

'As you know, the coroner's inquest is to be resumed on Friday. Dental evidence of the man's identity will be produced and you, Mr Ainger, have been called to attend and give evidence to account for his presence on your land, and to say what you know about him.'

Ainger cleared his throat and nodded solemnly. Typical of the man, Quantrill thought, to come dressed in his clerical grey; difficult to disbelieve a man in a dog-collar.

'The autopsy has been completed,' went on the Chief Inspector, 'but it provided no evidence as to the cause of death. It's not for me to anticipate the coroner's conclusion, but in the circumstances it's likely that he will bring in an open verdict. Athol Garrity's remains will be buried—by you next Monday, I believe, Mr Ainger—and the file will be closed.'

He could almost swear that he heard the Aingers give a joint sigh of relief. Certainly they stirred in their chairs, and their tension slackened.

Quantrill leaned forward across his desk. 'However—' he said sharply, and he saw with satisfaction that Mrs Ainger flinched, '—a closed file can be reopened at any time if new evidence comes to light. And frankly I'm not satisfied that, in the course of my enquiries, I've heard the whole truth. I am convinced that someone in Breckham Market knows more than he—or she—has told me so far. And withholding information from the police is a very serious offence.'

He sat back in his chair and waited, watching them. They avoided his eyes, and also each other's. Gillian's cheeks had reddened, and the knuckles of her clasped hands were white. Robin's hands were hidden in the pockets of his jacket, but his face was drained of colour. The silence in the room, Quantrill thought, was thick enough to cut and butter.

'Look,' he said suddenly, softening his voice and attitude. 'I have a theory about Garrity's death. I've heard from various sources that he wasn't a particularly prepossessing young man—noisy, foul-mouthed, and quite a heavy drinker. Now, let's suppose that he behaved offensively last summer, and that someone knocked him down. His opponent would probably then leave him and walk off, thinking that Garrity would pick himself up later. But instead, because he'd been drinking heavily, he choked and was asphyxiated by his own vomit. That can happen quite easily, you know—it's why, when we lock up drunks in the cells here, an officer has to look at them every half-hour to make sure they're all right.

'But when his opponent discovered that Garrity was dead, he must have panicked. My guess is that he hid the body, after dark, in the bushes at the bottom of Parson's Close, thinking—because he knew that the tenant farmer no longer used that field—that it wouldn't be found. He hid the tent, too; hid it, or sold it, or gave it away—anything to get rid of it. And ever since then, he's had to live with a man's death on his conscience. He's been afraid to confess, partly because of the damage it would do to his career and partly because he doesn't want the real reason for his quarrel with Garrity to be made public. I think I can guess what that reason is, but it needn't concern us here.'

Silent tears had begun to slide down Gillian Ainger's face, and now she gave a gasping sob. Her husband reached out for her hand and clasped it tightly, but they neither looked at each other nor spoke.

'If my theory is anywhere near right,' went on Quantrill quietly, 'I want anyone who was involved to know that as long as he admits to what he did, there will be no need for the details of his quarrel with Garrity to come out in open court. And whatever may happen to his career if he confesses, I think that he and his family will be able to live more happily in the future than they have done since Athol Garrity's death.'

The Aingers said nothing, but Gillian was crying openly now and Quantrill felt confident that she would talk if she were on her own. He sent Robin Ainger into an adjoining office under escort, lit a small cigar for himself and offered a cigarette to the Rector's wife. She shook her head.

'Why are you crying, Mrs Ainger?'

'You know what I have to contend with at home,' she said unsteadily, searching her bag for a handkerchief. 'I'm at my wits' end, trying to cope with Dad and the house-keeping as well as all the parish work...and now this.' Her face was ugly, her eyelids swollen and her mouth gar-goyled with the attempt to hold back her sobs. 'You've been badgering us unmercifully, Mr Quantrill. Do you wonder I'm crying?'

'It wasn't my intention to make you cry, but I'm not surprised. You're unhappy and pressured and frightened, and I think you'll crack up if you don't confide in some-one. So please tell me what you know about Garrity's death. It's difficult for you, I realize that, but you'd do better to confess and suffer a quick burst of adverse pub-licity rather than to go on living in this state of permanent tension. Come on, get it off your conscience. The courts can be remarkably lenient, you know.'

She put away her handkerchief. Her voice was clogged with emotion, but she spoke with dignity: 'I—I have nothing to say.'

Sympathy and gentleness were getting him nowhere. 'Mrs Ainger,' he said more sharply, stubbing out his cigar, 'you must understand the seriousness of my enquiry. I have reason to believe that you can give me some infor-mation as to the circumstances of Athol Garrity's death. Now tell me: what do you know about it?'

He watched her in the ensuing silence, his eyes as green and hard as little apples. Her own red-rimmed eyes blinked, but when she spoke again her voice had regained all the firmness and authority of a parson's wife with six-teen years' experience of dealing with disaffected parish-ioners.

'I'm sorry, Chief Inspector, but I have nothing more to say.'

Baulked, but determined to use every tactic he knew, Quantrill sent her out to wait with a policewoman in another office, and had the Rector brought in.

'Now, Mr Ainger,' he said, standing formidably behind his desk. 'I've talked to your wife and she has given me her version of the circumstances surrounding Athol Garrity's death. Now I want to hear, in your own words, exactly what happened.'

For a moment, the Rector's handsome face sagged. He glanced doubtfully, anxiously, towards the door that led into the corridor down which he had glimpsed his wife being escorted. He swallowed nervously, and then his face began to clear.

'I have nothing to say,' he said.

Quantrill glared at him, his frustration mounting. He had put so much conviction into his hypothetical account of Athol Garrity's death that he had almost persuaded himself that he knew it to be true. Now he remembered, with reluctance, that in fact he knew nothing; not even that a crime had been committed.

Well, he'd gone too far to draw back. Might as well go all the way. If the Aingers were innocent, they had behaved remarkably suspiciously, and he had almost sufficient justification for the question he was about to put. Even if it led to a complaint from Ainger to the Chief Constable, he intended to put it.

'Mr Ainger,' he said slowly, 'a young man you knew, a man you have entertained at the Rectory, has died in unexplained circumstances, and the body has been found on your land. You've already told me something about him, and you've been frank enough to tell me that you disliked him, but my information suggests that you know more than you've said. I am going to put a question to you and I expect you, as a man of God, to answer me fully and truthfully. Did you have any part in, or are you in any way an accessory to, Athol James Garrity's death?'

The Rector's eyes were a vivid, unfocused blue. He hesitated for a moment, and then said loudly and clearly, 'I can tell you nothing more.'

'County operations room, Inspector Tait here.'

'Quantrill, Breckham. The inquest's over: verdict open, file closed. I tried to get an admission from the Aingers but they wriggled out of it.'

'Oh, for God's sake! Didn't you—?'

'Don't let's hold another inquest. I went as far as I could—a lot further than I should have done, considering we've no evidence of a crime—but they were obviously expecting something of the sort and they came prepared. I spoke to them together and separately, but I got nowhere.'

'I knew that I should have been there.'

'What the hell do you think you could have done that I didn't? They're not thick, they're an intelligent couple who knew why they'd been sent for and had planned exactly what they were going to say. But I'm not going to leave it at that. They know now that I'm suspicious of them, and I'm going to try to rattle them by letting them see that they're being watched. And for a start, I'm going to watch the Reverend Robin bury what's left of Athol Garrity. Monday morning, nine-thirty at the town cemetery. If you're not on duty, do you want to come?'

'*Now* you ask me,' complained Inspector Tait.

'Suit yourself,' snapped Chief Inspector Quantrill, and slammed down the receiver.

# Chapter 13

On Sunday night, winter returned briefly to East Anglia. A cold northerly airstream lowered the temperature sharply. Freezing fog gathered, shrouding every hedge and tree so closely that when it dispersed in the early hours it left clinging deposits of rime.

By nine-fifteen on Monday morning, with the low sun shining from a cloudless sky, the landscape was a dazzling white. Hoar frost filigreed every twig and frond, making Breckham Market cemetery seem, for the space of an hour or two, ethereal.

Quantrill chose to arrive early, driving along the infelicitously named Cemetery Road with the sun visor down to keep some of the blinding brightness out of his eyes. The road was semi-rural, used only by local traffic, and the Chief Inspector was able to park close to the cemetery gates, immediately behind the Rector's Morris 1300. His companion, Detective Constable Ian Wigby, got out and went to talk to a cub reporter from the local newspaper, who was loitering for the purpose of extracting as much lineage as possible from his *Skeleton in Parson's Close: Mystery Man from Down Under* story. Quantrill was about to walk through the gates when he saw that Gillian Ainger's father, Henry Bowers, was huddled in the back of the Rectory car.

It was persistence rather than kindness that prompted Quantrill to speak to the old man. Henry Bowers might be decrepit but he was not gaga, and according to Martin Tait he had been lively enough the previous summer. There was a chance that he might be able to remember something useful about the Australian, and Quantrill was determined to cover every possibility before he finally admitted defeat.

He opened the driver's door and put his head inside the car. "Morning, Henry.'

The old man was sitting slack as a turtle inside the gaping neck of his heavy overcoat, staring vacantly into space and sucking a peppermint. When Quantrill addressed him, his body jerked with surprise and his mouth fell open.

'Sorry,' apologized the Chief Inspector. 'Didn't mean to startle you. Remember me—Doug Quantrill? We had a drink together at the Boot a few weeks ago.'

'Oh ar?' mumbled Henry Bowers uneasily. He peered up through the bristle of his eyebrows, wiped his damp mouth and shifted his peppermint into the opposite cheek. 'I know, you're the copper. Bought me a nice drop o' whisky...but I didn't talk, did I? Didn't let the family down.'

'No, you didn't let them down,' Quantrill agreed. He sat himself behind the wheel and closed the door against the cold, turning sideways to talk to the old man. 'You're up and about early today.'

Henry Bowers nodded. 'Got to go to the health centre this morning,' he said importantly. 'Got to be fitted for a truss. Our Gillian's going to take me as soon as they've finished the funeral.'

'Is your daughter here?' said Quantrill, surprised.

'Ar. They're burying the Aussie, and he's got no

relations over here so they thought they'd both go. Looks better that way. Looks as though they cared.'

'And do they?'

The old man fumbled about in his pocket and produced a pack of peppermints. His shaky fingers had difficulty in tearing the wrapping, and Quantrill had to restrain himself from taking over. 'Do they care about the Australian's death?' he persisted.

'Not them. Why should they? Bloody good riddance, if you ask me. Want a peppermint?'

'Not just now, thanks. Look, Henry, I need to know how that man died.'

'That's no secret, now the coroner's sat on him. All that fizzy canned beer he drank…probably choked hisself to death. That's what it said in the *Daily Press*.' He put another mint, with a piece of wrapper still adhering to it, into his mouth.

'Yes, but I want to know what he was doing just before he died. Was he by any chance at the Rectory?'

Henry Bowers's watery eyes were suddenly shrewd. 'Didn't think you knew for sure when he did die. Not according to the paper.'

'We don't. I'm talking about the day when he was last seen, July the 29th last year.'

'Oh ar. Well, the Aussie wouldn't have been at the Rectory then, because he'd told him to keep away, weeks before.'

'The Rector had told him?'

'Ar. They'd had a row—about brass-rubbing, or something o' the sort. Anyway, the Aussie didn't show his face after that. Bloody good job, too. Couldn't stand the feller. D'y know what he had the nerve to call me? *Grandad!* Bloody Aussie…' He sucked vigorously at his peppermint, looked surprised, slowly pushed out his tongue from between his dark lips, and picked off a fragment of wet wrapping-paper with the tough nails of his thumb and forefinger.

Quantrill stared at him thoughtfully. 'And what about you, Henry? Do *you* know anything about Athol Garrity's death?'

'I could ha' told you about that right from the start. Too much canned beer, that was his trouble. I told him it'd rot his guts.' The old man brightened, and pointed over Quantrill's shoulder at the approaching hearse. 'Here he comes! They've taken long enough to get him buried, eh? It's weeks since they found him.'

'He came to no harm while he waited,' said Quantrill drily. He opened the car door. The conversation, like most of the others he'd had concerning the Australian, had been tantalizingly inconclusive. 'All right, then, Henry,' he said. 'Mind what you get up to.'

'Better take a peppermint,' suggested the old man. 'It's always cold enough to perish you in that cemetery.'

Quantrill helped himself from the proffered pack. Henry Bowers was looking not at him but at the hearse as it turned in through the gates. He had on his face a look of sly glee that the Chief Inspector had once or twice before noticed on old people who watched their juniors being buried; presumably a manifestation of triumph at the thought that they had outlived someone younger and stronger. Such childishness was one of the aspects of ageing that Quantrill, at forty-seven, found particularly unattractive. He had long ago decided that he himself would prefer not to live much beyond seventy, although he had sufficient imagination to concede that he might, once he passed sixty, begin revising his idea of what constituted a ripe old age.

He pocketed the peppermint, nodded to Henry

Bowers, shut the car door behind him and walked through the cemetery gates. The hearse was travelling decorously up the gravelled centre path, and the Chief Inspector took a short cut over the frosted grass, between two rows of tall white marble Victorian headstones, to reach the area that was in current use.

There were more people present than he had anticipated. Martin Tait had come, and was standing with DC Wigby a short distance from the newly dug grave. The verger of St. Botolph's, Edgar Blore, stood in his black cassock on the far side of the grave, with the newspaper reporter, and the man who lived in the lodge at the cemetery gates and trebled as the town's park-keeper, gardener, and gravedigger.

The Reverend Robin Ainger, looking like a '30s film star in the full-length black winter cloak that he wore over his surplice, was waiting beside the path for the coffin to be removed from the hearse. At the graveside, where the relatives would normally stand, were Gillian Ainger and a man of about fifty who looked, with his neatly brushed greying hair, gold-rimmed glasses, and tailored overcoat, like a successful professional adviser.

''Morning, Martin,' Quantrill said as he joined the other policemen. 'Do either of you know the man with Mrs Ainger?'

'No,' said Wigby, 'but I thought we ought to, so I asked the verger. His name's Reynolds. Don't know his occupation, but he lives somewhere near Yarchester. He's been over here on Sundays quite often during the past six months—he goes to Evensong with Mrs Ainger.'

'He's either a very good friend,' said Tait, 'or a solicitor. I don't see what he's doing out here so early on a Monday morning otherwise.'

The three policemen looked across the intervening

low modern headstones at Gillian Ainger and her companion, and were interested to see that she was conscious of their presence. She turned her head to say something urgent to Reynolds, and then moved her position so that she was partly masked from their view by the frost-candied branches of a rose-bush. But they could see enough to observe Reynolds stepping closer to her, and putting a hand under her elbow.

Wigby slapped his sheepskin-gloved hands together. 'Either a very friendly solicitor, or a very solicitous friend,' he suggested breezily. Tait, the shorter man, contrived to look down his nose at him.

'I see what you mean, sir,' he said to Quantrill. 'Gillian certainly seems worried about us.'

'I'd give a lot to know why,' said the Chief Inspector. He reconsidered his offer in the light of his bank balance, and made a hasty amendment. 'At least, I'd be prepared to make a small donation to the church restoration fund out of my own pocket.' He took off his hat and nudged Ian Wigby to do the same; with nothing in the coffin but bones, and no mourning relatives to consider, the detective constable had temporarily forgotten the proprieties.

Preceded by the Rector, the bearers carried the coffin towards the grave. The burial expenses of the stranger were having to be met by the local ratepayers, and so the ceremony was being performed as cheaply as possible. Quantrill approved of it that way, not only in the interests of economy but because it was simple and traditional. The undertaker was a small Breckham builder and joiner, who made coffins as an extension of his trade. He wore the same black suit that he had worn at funerals for the past thirty years, and his hearse was a vintage Daimler; the bearers were his workmen, taken off their regular work for an hour to put on suits and shoulder the coffin.

'At least he's nice and light,' muttered Ian Wigby irreverently, as Athol Garrity's scant remains were lowered easily into the grave.

The Reverend Robin Ainger, hearing the remark on the still frosty air, hesitated in the middle of *Man that is born of woman hath but a short time to live.* He looked up, and for the first time noticed the stolid row of policemen watching him. He resumed almost immediately, but his recital was mechanical; he glanced anxiously at his wife while he repeated the next two verses, then faltered over *Thou knowest, Lord, the secrets of our hearts.* All three policemen stared at him, willing him to go on, and he seemed to pull himself together. The verger stepped forward to cast earth on the coffin, and Ainger finished the committal service in a firm voice and record time, with his breath going up like smoke in the cold air.

As soon as he decently could, Quantrill clapped his hat back on his head and put Henry Bowers's peppermint into his mouth. As the old man had said, the cemetery was perishingly cold. He watched Robin Ainger and the man called Reynolds walk away briskly, one on either side of Gillian, their feet crunching on the whitened grass. The gravedigger moved in immediately to complete his work, and frozen lumps of earth began to thud down on the coffin.

'Well, what did you make of it, Martin?' asked Quantrill as he began to move towards the gate. But Inspector Tait lingered, studying a new headstone that had caught his eye.

'Michael Dade,' Tait said. 'Wasn't he the church organist? I met him last summer, and he died in October...that would have been just after I got my promotion and moved to Yarchester. Thirty-one when he died...what was it, an accident?'

'Suicide,' said DC Wigby. 'He was disappointed in love, so he put a plastic bag over his head.'

'I met him just once, at the Rectory,' said Tait. 'A small dark nervy man, with a big nose and a bad stammer.'

'That was him,' said Wigby. He corrected Tait with relish: '*Deputy* organist at the church, though. I did the enquiry into his death—you won't remember it, Mr. Quantrill, you were on leave at the time. He got it into his head that some foreign girl had promised to marry him, but then she went off. He kept hoping that she'd come back, or at least write to him, but she didn't. He finally gave up, wrote a note telling his widowed mother to look after herself, put the bag over his head and died of asphyxia. It was a perfectly straightforward case of suicide.'

'Who was the girl?' asked Tait.

'Ah, that I didn't find out. According to his mother she was a student at Yarchester. Not that his poor old Mum had ever set eyes on her, because Michael didn't take her home. And he had no real friends, so he didn't confide in anyone.'

'But what was the girl's name?' said Tait impatiently.

'His Mum's deaf, and didn't ever catch it. I wouldn't be surprised if the love affair was mostly in Michael's imagination. He was a pathetic little sod, still living at home, still doing the same clerical job he'd had ever since he left school, too shy and too much of a stammerer to attract girls.'

'But did you say that this girl was a foreign student at Yarchester?' asked Quantrill. He turned to Tait. 'I suppose it couldn't have been—?'

'I think it was,' said Tait, his voice tight and eager. 'He was at the Rectory when I met Janey Rolph. He was obviously besotted by her, hanging about hoping for a look or a kind word. Not that she seemed to give him any encouragement, but as Wigby says it could have been all in his mind. It certainly fits as far as timing is concerned. I know that Janey was due to leave this country at the end of July. Michael Dade killed himself in October. That means he spent three months waiting and hoping to hear from her before he gave up. Yes, it fits.'

'Holy cow,' said the Chief Inspector slowly, though without attempting his son's impression of an Australian accent. 'So one young man who visited the Rectory last year has died in unexplained circumstances, another has committed suicide. The parson and his wife are feeling and acting guilty, their friend Reynolds is obviously supporting them, Gillian's father is being as obstructive as they are—and there's not a damn thing we can do about it because we've no idea what really happened. What in heaven's name *did* go on at that Rectory last summer?'

# Part 2—Last Summer

# Chapter 14

**G**illian Ainger had been married for nearly sixteen years, and during the whole of that time she had never once thought to ask herself whether her marriage was happy. Over the years she had come to have increasingly frequent private doubts about her role as a parson's wife, and about the faith she professed, but none at all about her husband. Quite simply, she loved him.

That he—handsome, strong, clever, much admired—should choose to marry her rather than a prettier, livelier girl was for Gillian a continuing source of wonder. They had met as students at King's College, London. Robin Ainger, then twenty-three, was completing a post-graduate theological course, and Gillian had just begun her pre-clinical medical training. She was eighteen. She knew herself to be shy and plain, and she couldn't understand why Robin sought her company in preference to that of the more attractive girls who vied for his attention. Having gone to university with no thought, let alone expectation, of acquiring anything other than her medical qualifications, she was dazzled to find herself, a year later, with a newly ordained parson for a husband.

It was idealism that had made her choose medicine as a career, but she gave up her course without any misgivings in order to accompany Robin when he went as curate to a large Hertfordshire parish. She had never been more than conventionally religious, but love, coming to her as a revelation, had so heightened her perceptions and liberated her senses that it seemed to her that it must, in its widest interpretation as the gospel of Christianity, be the answer to everything. Accordingly she didn't abandon her idealism, but merely changed its course. She had always wanted to do something worthy with her life, and helping Robin with his cure of souls seemed to her a vocation every bit as valid as devoting herself to the cure of bodies.

'You'll make an ideal parson's wife,' Robin had assured her when at first she voiced her doubts, and she had gradually come to believe that this must be true. Why else should he want to marry her?

'Because I love you, of course.'

'But *why* do you love me, Robin?'

'Because you're good and kind and sweet...and impossibly innocent. You need someone to look after you.'

That was what he believed. But his unacknowledged motive in marrying her, rather than one of the pretty girls who clustered round him like wasps round a jampot, was in fact more fundamental. Robin Ainger was afraid of wasps.

Pretty girls—competitive, insistent, demanding girls—terrified him. His mother had spoiled him, and had encouraged a self-centredness that made it essential for him to marry someone who would bolster his feeling of superiority, and at the same time cosset and protect him. Young as she was, Gillian made a perfect mother-substitute, and Robin loved her for it; not so much for herself, as for herself in relation to him.

But he was not a man who attempted any self-analysis, and so this aspect of his relationship with Gillian escaped him. Instead, he prided himself that in choosing her he had looked beyond superficialities and recognized Gillian's true worth. This made him feel strong and protective. He failed to acknowledge, because he failed to realize, how much he needed her and depended on her. And Gillian, enslaved by his good looks and grateful for his love, prepared to devote her life to helping him in his work without understanding that she was by far the stronger and abler of the two.

The first twelve years of their marriage were happy, chiefly because they instinctively avoided introspection and discussion. They were content simply to live and work together, moving from one benefice to a better as the opportunity arose. Their only disappointment in those years was the non-appearance of children, but their sorrow was more expressed than real: Gillian was quite busy enough coping with Robin, and the moves, and parish affairs, without having babies; and Robin wanted no rivals for her attention.

The demands of a large parish were greater than either of them had realized. Robin, whose father was a scholar by inclination, had been brought up in a quiet country rectory. No scholar himself, and anxious for preferment, he had deliberately sought busier and more important benefices without at first appreciating how total his dedication would have to be. And Gillian, anxious as she was to involve herself, was alarmed to find that as the parson's wife she became in effect parish property. She had not expected to be so universally recognized, so much observed and discussed, so frequently in demand and yet so often criticized.

At first, this front-line feeling strengthened their marriage. After twelve years they were still very much a partnership; still prepared, whenever the pressures became too great, to say 'Drat the lot of them!' and sneak out of the parish like truant schoolchildren for a day off. Occasionally they would lock the doors, take the telephone receiver off its rest, and go to bed for an hour or two in the afternoon. There were, they agreed, so many disadvantages about working from home that they might as well make the most of the benefits.

But by the time they made their fourth move, to Breckham Market, their sense of partnership had begun to disintegrate. Had they been able to admit their personal difficulties and discuss them, instead of confining their conversation to domestic and parish affairs, they might have been able to help each other. As it was, they each tried to find their own solution without reference to the other.

For Robin Ainger, the problem was his faith. He had gone into the church not because of any sense of vocation but because his father and grandfather had been clergymen. It was the only way of life he knew. He had assumed without question that he had faith, but over the years it had diminished until it hardly existed at all. The words and phrases he uttered in church became increasingly meaningless to him.

The guilt this occasioned made him feel like a criminal. His instinctive response was concealment. He refused to think, let alone talk to his wife, about his loss of faith. The church was his livelihood and he enjoyed the status it gave him; as long as he continued to go through the motions, no one needed to know that he no longer believed in what he was saying.

And so he threw himself into the life of the parish and town, deliberately exhausting himself with overwork so as to avoid the leisure for thought. As for the church services, he got through them by putting increasing emphasis on form rather than content. While most churchmen were busily trying to make services more relevant by adopting modern forms of worship, Robin Ainger clung to the Authorized Version of the Bible and to the Book of Common Prayer. And while many believers, clerical and lay, spoke out in favour of allowing divorcees to remarry in church, Robin ducked the issue by adhering rigidly to the traditional Anglican discipline that Christian marriage is for life.

But while he expatiated on the sanctity of marriage, and believed himself to be setting a domestic example to his flock, his wife felt increasingly isolated. Her own religious faith, so radiant when she first married, had dimmed in a way that she felt to be totally unacceptable in a parson's wife, and she knew no method of reviving it. Going to church and listening to Robin's confident sonority made her feel wretchedly guilty. She longed to opt out, but that was impossible; the parish would be scandalized.

For herself, she wouldn't have cared. Her idealism had turned to disillusionment. Gillian was sick of the parish. Sick of the Mothers' Union and the Young Wives and the Sunday School, of arranging the flower-arrangers and organizing choir treats, of inspiring fund-raising events and sorting out catering problems. Sick of petty controversies, of bickering, and of the appallingly un-Christian lack of charity manifested by some of the most faithful members of the congregation. Sick of the procession of callers at the Rectory, of the sound of the telephone bell, of the absence of privacy.

But she had to keep going, because of Robin. He was working so hard that she couldn't worry him with her personal problems and uncertainties, let alone lay any extra burdens on him by neglecting her parish duties. After all, she loved him.

It was, though, becoming increasingly difficult to talk to him. Tiredness made Robin irritable, and when he was irritable he would slap down any attempt she made at conversation, ridiculing her into silence. Disagreement infuriated him. She did not side with him on a number of issues—divorce, for one—but she knew that he resented any intervention in what he believed to be his province, and so she kept quiet. The confidence that, over the years, she had of necessity acquired in dealing with parishioners did not extend to her relationship with her husband. She tried to avert his displeasure by being apologetic, not realizing that this only made him more overbearing.

And the trouble was that she had no one else to talk to. She knew scores of people in Breckham Market, but because she was the wife of the Rector there wasn't a single person in whose company she felt she could let her hair down. Gillian Ainger was intolerably lonely.

In the sixteenth year of her marriage, she could bear the isolation no longer. She made up her mind that—in defiance of her husband if necessary—she would set about finding herself some friends.

'But why Yarchester? Why waste petrol by going all that way? There are plenty of evening classes you can join here in Breckham Market.'

'Yes, I know...but that's just the trouble, Robin, don't you see? I feel that I want to get away from the parish sometimes.'

'Do you think that I don't feel the same?' he demanded. 'I'd be only too glad to get away for one evening a week, if I could spare the time.' He sliced the top off his breakfast boiled egg. 'Try one of the local classes,' he instructed her. He poked with his spoon at the semi-liquid contents of the eggshell. 'Cookery or something.'

'Isn't it done enough? Oh, I'm sorry, Robin. I'll boil you another—'

'Never mind. Leave it, for goodness' sake, I'll swallow it somehow. Your father will be down in a minute and I want to have at least one meal a day in peace.'

The habit of placating her husband had become so deeply ingrained that at any time before this morning Gillian would have taken his hint and said no more. Now, although her heart was beating faster than usual, she persisted.

'The thing is, you see, that I want to do sculpture and there are no classes for it at Breckham. I started it when we lived in Bedford, don't you remember? I modelled a head, and I've still got all the materials up in the attic—'

He looked up irritably. 'The circumstances then were different. We were only ten minutes' walk from the art school. Going to Yarchester would take all evening—and supposing I want the car?'

'The sculpture classes are on Tuesdays. You don't use the car then because you're taking confirmation classes here at the Rectory.'

Robin Ainger glared at his wife, his irritation mounting. They had almost always spent their leisure time together, and he resented her sudden bid for independence. 'You've got this all planned, haven't you?' he accused her.

She went pink. 'I've tried to anticipate the possible snags, that's all. I don't want to make things difficult for you.'

'What about your father, then? What am I supposed to do with him while you're gadding about in Yarchester?'

'He's no trouble in the evenings, as long as you let him watch his favourite television programmes. I can leave a cold supper for you both—'

'Thanks very much.'

'—or I could cook you a high tea before I go, scrambled eggs or something. Whatever you like, Robin. Only you won't mind if I go to these classes, will you?'

His handsome face was dark with annoyance. 'Frankly, Gillian, I'd have thought you could find enough to do here without wasting time and money by going to Yarchester to play about with clay.'

He would have been a great deal angrier, Gillian reflected guiltily, had he known her real reason for wanting to go to Yarchester. She could hardly believe that he didn't know, because she was planning what he—and she—regularly counselled lonely parishioners to do. Get out more, they both advised: if you want to meet people, the best way to do it is to join a club or take up a hobby.

She had often wondered, as she trotted out the conventional wisdom, whether in fact it ever worked on any but the most superficial level. Did the exchange of platitudes that passed for conversation at all the Breckham clubs, from the Mothers and Toddlers to the Over-Sixties, really make lonely people feel befriended, or did it merely emphasize their sense of isolation? And could communal participation in yoga or cookery or clay modelling possibly be expected to ensure a meeting of kindred spirits?

As Tuesday evening approached, that began to seem more and more unlikely. She set out for Yarchester School of Art—seen off by her husband with a short, huffed,

'Mind how you go'—knowing that it was unrealistic to hope to acquire anything from the course apart from a plaster cast of the head she proposed to model. And for the first two weeks it seemed that she was wise not to be optimistic.

There were a number of women on the course, and they were friendly enough in the larky way that some adults automatically adopt when they return to a classroom environment, but she found it difficult to know how to become better acquainted. She had chafed at the pressures and expectations that were put on her because she was the wife of the Rector of Breckham Market, but once she got away from the town and lost that identity she felt as shy as she had been in adolescence. She had joined the course late, and this made her feel an outsider. When the man next to her on the bench, who had introduced himself as Alec Reynolds and had found some clean clay for her to use instead of the plaster-filled lump the instructor gave her, suggested after her third lesson that she might like to go with some members of the class for a drink at a nearby pub, she was so lacking in self-confidence that she almost refused.

Had she refused, and gone straight back home to her husband, Breckham Market cemetery would today be three graves emptier; possibly four.

# Chapter 15

It would have been impossible for anyone to warn Gillian Ainger of the likely consequence of her attempt to make friends, because she wouldn't have believed it.

She was a straightforward, rational woman; not without imagination or sensitivity, but with no significant depth of emotion. Love, to her, was something basic and enduring, and passion was no more than the occasional physical expression of love. She knew nothing of the terrors of insecurity, of the desperation of dependence, of possessiveness, of destructiveness, of black jealousy, of murderous hatred, of the darkness of the soul. As her husband had recognized from the first, Gillian was an innocent.

She had no idea how fiercely possessive Robin felt about her. When they exchanged their wedding vows, promising to forsake all others, Gillian had meant—and had assumed that Robin also meant—that she was forswearing extramarital love affairs. It had never occurred to her that Robin took her promise literally, and that when he said, as he was accustomed to say when they made love, 'You're mine, mine,' he meant that she belonged to him absolutely and that she must never give anything of herself to anyone else.

Gillian hadn't been a parson's wife for sixteen years

without becoming aware of the depressing incidence in every parish of gossip, malice, slander, hypocrisy, fornication, and adultery, but she still preferred to think the best of everyone. She took the view that most of the crimes that were committed in Breckham Market, from vandalism to wife-battering, were attributable to a combination of under-privilege and inadequacy. She never had the time or interest to read newspaper accounts of criminal cases, and so to discover that what powers the foulest of crimes is very often love.

As a regular churchgoer at traditional services, she was well acquainted with the Litany. Some of it she found appropriate to the last quarter of the twentieth century, but other sections seemed to her to be completely outdated. In making the ancient supplication, *From all evil and mischief; from sin, from the crafts and assaults of the devil; from thy wrath and from everlasting damnation, Good Lord deliver us,* Gillian Ainger was comfortably unaware of the ever-present existence of the power of evil.

But that was before she deliberately set out to make friends outside the parish, and took Alec Reynolds and Janey Rolph home to meet her husband.

Reynolds had been a widower for three years. He had loved his late wife very dearly, and the reason he took an interest in Gillian was that she reminded him in many ways of Sylvia.

He was not looking for anything other than friendship, because he was now emotionally attached to a civil-service colleague whose career had recently taken her to live and work in London. She reserved most, though not all, of her weekends for Alec Reynolds, but during the week he was always a widower again.

'I never have a dull moment,' he told Gillian as she

drank the bitter lemon he had bought her. He spoke cheerfully, but his eyes behind the gold-rimmed glasses were bleak, still grieving for the happy home life that Sylvia had created. Now, with the children married, the house was empty and neglected; the only attraction there was the whisky bottle. Going out as much as possible during the Monday-to-Friday six-to-midnight wasteland helped to cut down the amount of time he had to spend trying to resist temptation.

His pastimes, though, were not chosen haphazardly. Alcohol, which had never had much appeal for him when his wife was alive, had, he discovered, a dangerous effect on him. The first two glasses were enjoyably anaesthetizing, but after that there would begin a slow-burning rage at the malignant fate that had taken Sylvia from him. Then violence was liable to erupt, because Alec Reynolds in drink was not the mild, urbane man that his appearance suggested. On more than one occasion he had swept his arm across the kitchen table, sending his unwashed dishes and the remains of his Bird's Eye pizza-for-one crashing to the floor. Once, he had flung an empty bottle through the television screen. And so he had wisely opted for pastimes that would not merely keep him occupied but challenge and tire him: Russian lessons mentally, squash and sculpture physically.

'Don't you find sculpture tough going?' he asked Gillian.

'It's rather like all-in wrestling,' she agreed, laughing. 'All that twisting of metal to make the armature, and then pounding the clay about and slapping it on…' Her hands, he noticed, were square and blunt and not well cared-for. They didn't attract him, as Lesley's slim, manicured hands did, but they looked steady and capable; like Sylvia's.

He told her about Sylvia, and also about Lesley and

her disinclination to abandon her career and settle down as the wife of a provincial senior civil servant. In return, Gillian told him something about her own life, with the doubts and all but the most superficial problems edited out.

She found Alec Reynolds pleasant and sympathetic, the kind of person she'd hoped for as a friend, someone with whom she might eventually be able to discuss her difficulties. She had assumed that any friends she made would be women, but she could see no objection to befriending a man as long as she was open about it, and invited him home as soon as possible so that her husband could get to know him too. Robin might protest about having his privacy disturbed, but she was sure that he would find it as liberating as she did to be able to talk to someone who had no connection with Breckham Market, or with clerical life.

For a woman who had been married for so long, Gillian Ainger knew dangerously little about her husband.

Minutes later, she made a second friend.

Reynolds had left her to make a promised telephone call to Lesley, and Gillian was about to talk to one of the other sculptors when a tall young man, with a voice as harsh as a kookaburra, lurched sideways and bumped against her, spilling beer on her coat.

He didn't seem to notice, but a vividly red-haired girl who was near him came immediately to Gillian's rescue, trying to brush off the wetness. 'I'm *sorry*,' she said. Her accent was slighter and softer than the man's, but identifiably Australian. 'I really am sorry.'

'It wasn't your fault. Don't worry, the coat will take no harm.'

'Can I get you a drink, to compensate?' The girl glanced disparagingly at the lanky, loose-jawed man who was regaling some Suffolk youths with an Antipodean dirty story. 'I'll persuade Athol to pay, of course, but I'm afraid it's no use hoping he'll make the offer. What will you have?'

'Thank you, but I won't. I really was just leaving.'

'Oh, *please.*' The girl seemed distressed. Her eyes, set wide in her delicately boned face, were big with hurt. 'Don't turn me down. I couldn't bear it if you went away thinking that *all* Australians are uncouth. Some of us are quite civilized, if only you'll give us a chance to show it. My name's Janey Rolph, by the way.'

Her striking looks had turned nearly every male head in the bar, but she seemed totally unconscious of the interest she created. All her attention was focused on Gillian who, too kind-hearted to snub her, introduced herself and accepted another bitter lemon.

'I really mustn't stay long, though,' said Gillian. 'I live in a market town half an hour's drive away, and I didn't tell my husband I'd be late.'

'I was brought up in a small town too, not far—well, seventy miles—from Brisbane,' said Janey. 'Would you believe Birmingham, population just over a thousand? It's Athol Garrity's home town as well. I've been over here eighteen months, post-grad at the U. Athol's backpacking round Europe, and he turned up in Yarchester a couple of weeks ago looking for floor space for his bedroll. I couldn't refuse, and now it's difficult to get rid of him. He's really embarrassing. Here am I trying to live down the crude Australian image, while he's doing his best to reinforce it.'

'And are you enjoying the university?' asked Gillian. 'How's the research going?'

The girl's mouth took a wry downturn. 'Slowly. Working for an M. Phil. is an isolating experience. That's why I was quite glad to see Athol again, for the first fifteen minutes anyway. Apart from a discussion with my supervisor twice a term, I'm entirely on my own. That can be very depressing, especially in winter. I hate your winters. Low grey skies give me claustrophobia.'

Janey shuddered. For a moment she looked fragile with cold and loneliness and homesickness, but then she made an effort to be positive. 'Now that winter's over, though, I'm beginning to feel better. You can't imagine what a revelation my first English spring, last year, was. Spring in Australia comes overnight, somewhere in the middle of October. Most of our trees are evergreen, you see. This slow unfolding of greenery and blossom in April and May is incredibly beautiful. I've been reading English literature all my life, but until last year I had no idea what your poets were going on about when they wrote in praise of spring.'

Gillian was surprised and touched to hear of such deprivation. She recommended the pastoral beauty of the Suffolk countryside round Breckham Market, adding, 'My husband's the Rector there. If ever you come out that way, you must call.'

She had never seen anyone's face so much transformed by such a simple invitation. Janey was joyful. '*May* I? Do you really mean it? Oh, beaut! I live in one of the student residences, and I've never yet been in an English home.'

'Good heavens, haven't you?' Gillian was shocked by the thought of the isolation the girl must have endured. Despite her disenchantment with the parish, she had not entirely lost the impulse to spread loving-kindness, and so she plunged on without hesitation: 'Then of course you must come! Do ring me, and we'll arrange something.' She scribbled her address and telephone number on the notepad that she carried in her handbag, tore off the sheet and gave it to Janey.

Then she checked, hearing Athol Garrity's raucous voice behind her. She didn't move in circles where obscenities were accepted in conversation, and she had no intention of extending her hospitality to anyone who used them so freely.

The girl, watching her, understood. 'Don't worry,' Janey reassured her. 'I'd love to come and visit you, but I certainly won't bring Athol with me. He's the last person I'd want to have around.'

Gillian assumed that it was natural delicacy that made Janey want to keep Athol away from Breckham Market Rectory, but Janey's reasons were quite different.

For all his boorishness, there wasn't a scrap of harm in Athol Garrity. He behaved with overweening masculinity because that was the social norm in Birmingham, Queensland, but he was as predictable and as relatively innocuous as a can of Fosters. Too many beers, whether Fosters or Watneys, made him loutish; but he was never cunning or violent. He had no hidden depths.

But Janey Rolph had, and Athol knew it. He knew more about her background than Janey wanted anyone outside her home town to discover. Everyone in Birmingham, Queensland, knew that Janey's father, as a young man, had driven his car to the edge of the outback, abandoned it, disappeared for three weeks, and had then emerged, bearded and unrecognized, to join in the search for himself. Everyone knew that Janey, as a small child, had watched her paternal grandmother chase her grandfather round the yard with a carving-knife. Everyone knew that Janey's mother, before finally leaving her husband, had made more than one attempt to take her own life.

What no one could be sure of was the effect that this background had had on Janey. She was attractive, she was charming, she was brilliantly clever; she was also potentially dangerous. Everyone who met her liked her, but anyone who knew the instability on both sides of her family would be wary of becoming too closely involved with her. Athol Garrity was one of many men who were fascinated by her, but the only one outside Queensland who knew better than to trust her.

# Chapter 16

**A**lec Reynolds went to supper at Breckham Market Rectory on the following Monday evening. The occasion was not a success.

Robin had been stiff with hurt and rising panic when Gillian suggested it. He had suspected that something like this was in the air, from the moment when she returned from her class more than an hour late, looking happier and more animated than for a very long time. He had no doubt what had caused the change. She must have found someone else. He was going to lose her.

Fear and anger made him lash at her with his voice. 'It isn't appropriate for a married woman—particularly for a clergyman's wife—to make friends with another man.'

'That's exactly why I want to bring him home. I hope he'll become your friend too. And you needn't imagine,' she added with an unusual flash of spirit, 'that he has any designs on me, because he made a point of telling me that he has a woman friend he's hoping to marry. So you've no need to suspect his motives in our friendship, any more than mine.'

They had stood glaring at each other, Gillian guilty with new-found defiance, Robin furious with mistrust, both of them aware of the way the ground was crumbling beneath their feet.

'I shall see him in Yarchester when I go to my classes,

anyway,' pointed out Gillian. 'If you prefer me to do that—'

'Bring him, then, if you must,' he had snarled. 'Just don't expect me to welcome him, that's all!'

She should have had more sense, after that, she thought wryly, listening while her husband systematically quashed Alec's affable attempts at conversation, than to persist. On the other hand, she had never imagined that Robin could be so deliberately rude. Treating their guest as some kind of challenger, her husband was using all the weapons he could lay tongue to in an attempt to cut Reynolds's size. He was more tense than his wife had ever seen him. The muscles of his face tightened the skin so that it shone where the light caught it, and his pale blue eyes had a disturbingly unfocused gleam.

Gillian herself was so anxious about the relationship the men were failing to establish that she was unable to control the conversation. Her father tried to help, but his contribution was unattractive.

'A very nice bit o' chicken, dear,' he said to his daughter. He fingernailed a shred of meat from between two teeth. 'When I was at Gallipoli in 1915—' he began: he had spent only three days on the peninsula, at the age of eighteen, but he relived some part of the searing experience every day for the rest of his life, '—all we had to eat was bully beef. Rum ol' grub, in that climate in August. The ground was hot enough to scorch the soles o' your feet through your boots, and the bully beef was runny in the tins. More like soup. Half o' the battalion went down with dysentery—'

Understandably, Alec Reynolds refused to stay for coffee. Gillian walked dejectedly with him to his car, which he had parked in the drive. The clocks had recently changed, gaining an extra hour for summer time, and although the evening was still winter-cold there were pink bars of light in the sky behind the copper beech trees at the top of Parson's Close.

'I'm sorry, Alec,' she said. 'I shouldn't have invited you—I wouldn't have, if I'd known he'd be like this.'

Reynolds took off his glasses and polished them with his handkerchief. The atmosphere in the dining room, and the effort of remaining courteous, had made him sweat and smudged his lenses. Without them, he looked considerably less mild.

In fact he was blisteringly angry with Ainger for his rudeness, and vexed with Gillian for her naivety. He had accepted her invitation in good faith, expecting to spend a pleasant social evening with just such a relaxed and hospitable couple as he and Sylvia had been. But five minutes with the Aingers was enough to show him the direction and strength of Robin's emotions, and he was astonished that Gillian hadn't anticipated her husband's likely reaction. He put his glasses on again and opened the car door, anxious not to add to Ainger's suspicions by lingering too long.

'Surely you know that you're married to a very possessive man?' he said. 'Didn't you realize that you were asking for trouble by bringing another man home?'

'But that's juvenile!' she protested. 'It's uncivilized. Robin knows perfectly well that I love him. It's completely irrational of him to be upset.'

'My dear, reason doesn't come into it. Your husband can't help being possessive, anymore than your father can help being old. You'll never change him, and it's risky to try. Thank you for inviting me tonight, but it'll be in your best interests not to ask me here again.'

And not only in Gillian's interests, he thought. He had longed all evening to knock her husband down. He had never struck anyone in his adult life, but living alone had taught him that he was capable of lashing out. Although he had sat in the Rectory dining-room turning the other cheek in a civilized fashion, under the table his fists had been tightly clenched.

He had held back for Gillian's—for Sylvia's—sake, of course. He was able to hold back, because he had plenty of self-control as long as he was sober. But there was another consideration: prudence.

Reynolds was not at all sure how far his host's self-control extended. Difficult to tell, when he had not met the man before; difficult to assess, when the atmosphere was as highly charged with emotion as a circuit with electricity. But the strange, staring look in those eyes had alarmed Reynolds sufficiently to make him reluctant to tangle in any way with Robin Ainger.

He said a hasty good-bye to Gillian, backed out of the Rectory drive, and headed, thankfully for once, for his empty house.

From behind the half-drawn curtains of the darkened Rectory dining-room, Robin Ainger's pale eyes watched him go.

For the next hour or two the Aingers hardly spoke to one another.

Robin retreated to his study and sat at his desk with his head in his hands, raging silently over what he saw as Gillian's infidelity. She had not fallen in love with Reynolds—having seen them together, he realized that— nor Reynolds with her; but instead of easing his tension, this knowledge increased it.

Love, to Robin, was a passion that was total. Had his wife and Reynolds fallen in love, it would have seemed understandable; completely unforgivable, but at least involuntary. But he saw this easy friendship between his wife and another man, their ready conversation, the platonic pleasure that they evidently derived from each other's company, as a deliberate betrayal. If Gillian could do this to him, cynically repudiating what he saw as the totally exclusive nature of the marriage-bond, then she no longer loved him. He might not have lost her to Reynolds, but he had lost her in a way that was infinitely more destructive of his self-esteem.

Gillian, having washed up, stayed in the kitchen. She was furious with Robin for his rudeness, cross with herself for her inability to stand up to him, ashamed of the impression they had made on their guest. At the same time she was worried about Robin, anxious for his health because she knew that he was under stress, and guilty because she knew that she was contributing to his problems. But she had inherited from her father not only his lack of subtlety but also some of his peasant stubbornness. She was determined to persist with her classes in Yarchester and her new friendships, because she found it impossible to believe that Robin wouldn't soon get over his possessiveness and start to behave more sensibly.

But Robin, locked in his study, had been overwhelmed by the enormity of his wife's behaviour, and the desolation of losing her. He had put his head down on his desk and had begun to thump the side of his fist against the edge of the wood, rhythmically, viciously, until the skin broke and spots of blood flicked on to the pages of last night's sermon.

Soon after ten o'clock, Gillian heard his footfall in the tiled hall, and the creak of the downstairs cloakroom door. When he emerged, she called to him that she had just made coffee.

Robin followed his wife slowly into the kitchen. His face was pale and he smelled of antiseptic lotion. His damaged hand, wrapped in a handkerchief, was tucked into his trouser pocket. He took the mug she offered, mumbled an acknowledgement and, keeping his eyes averted from her, turned to walk away.

'Robin—'

He stood still with his back to her.

'Surely we can talk?'

'What is there to say?'

'You were rude to our guest, and spoiled my supper party. You could at least apologize.'

'I don't want to discuss it. Is the spare bed made up?'

She was jolted. In the whole of their married life they had never not shared their double bed. 'Oh—but—'

He shrugged. 'It doesn't matter. A couple of blankets will do.'

He followed her up the stairs. She went slowly, head down, feeling wretchedly confused. She hadn't bargained for such a rift. But perhaps Alec was right, perhaps Robin couldn't help himself. And however badly he behaved, she still loved him.

In the upstairs corridor she turned to him, lifting her head. 'I'm sorry,' she said. 'It was my fault, I should have known better than to invite him here. He means absolutely nothing to me, and I won't ask him again.'

Robin tried to focus his eyes on her, for the first time that evening. 'Really?' he asked with painful slowness.

'Really.' She lifted her hands and rested the palms lightly on his chest, close to the base of his throat. This was her accustomed prelude to offering him a kiss. After a moment, he bent his head and brushed his dry lips against her forehead. She could feel the too-rapid beat of his heart, the quiver of his chest against her hands, but his sketch of a kiss had reassured her.

'Really and truly,' she repeated, almost with gaiety. 'I'm certainly not going to quarrel with you over a friend.'

In her vocabulary, the word was completely innocuous. She had no idea why he stiffened and pulled away from her. 'Are you going to give up going to those classes?' he demanded in a tight voice.

'No, of course not. Not until they finish in May.'

'So you'll still see Reynolds?'

'Yes, at the classes. But good heavens—'

Her husband pushed her blindly aside, descended the stairs and began to drag on his coat. All his motions were exaggerated, as though he were sleepwalking. The handkerchief binding fell away from his hand, but he failed to notice.

Gillian ran down the stairs after him. 'Where are you going?'

'Do you care?' he spat, without looking at her. His face was a stranger's, older, uglier, the skin coarse and grey as lead. 'No, you don't, so don't lie to me. If you did care, you wouldn't go on hurting me like this.'

He went out of the door and slammed it behind him. A minute later she heard their car start up. He gunned the engine, she heard the squeal of rubber as he slewed the car out of the gates, and then he was off, shattering the quiet of St Botolph Street, driving as though all the devils in hell were at his shoulder.

# Chapter 17

Gillian was frightened.

She ran downstairs to pick up the handkerchief that Robin had dropped, saw the bloodstains, went to his study and found the spots of blood on his papers and the smears on the edge of his desk. It was not the injury itself that alarmed her. She knew that he could have accomplished little beyond bruising the flesh and breaking the skin. What horrified her was the violence with which he would have had to pound his hand against the wood before the skin broke, the passion that had caused him to do it, the insanity of the act. For those few moments, at least, her husband must have been out of his right mind.

She was not afraid for herself. But she was afraid for Robin, partly for his safety, partly for his sanity; and she was afraid for Alec Reynolds.

She rang Alec's number and blurted out her fears. He had been savouring a double whisky and reflecting philosophically that living alone had its compensations, and the urgency of her words startled him. He set about trying to reassure her as quickly as possible.

'I'm sure you've no need to worry, Gillian. Robin's probably just driving about until his head clears—he'll be all right. But if you're concerned about him, why not have a word with the police? No need to tell them what the problem is, you can say that he's been unwell and that he shouldn't be driving. They'd get their patrol cars to keep watch for him and make sure he gets home safely.'

There was an appalled silence from Gillian. Then, 'But Robin's the Rector of this parish. He'd never forgive me if I let him down like that.'

She told him then what she had hoped to be able to reveal gradually during the course of their friendship, about the pressures and problems of clerical life in a small community. 'That's why I've so much enjoyed coming to Yarchester, to get away from it all. But if Robin's going to let it upset him as much as this, I'll have to stop.'

Reynolds was genuinely sorry, but his chief concern at that moment was to get his doors locked and his house lights off. He said a few more words of reassurance and concluded, 'But if you're still worried, ring me again, whatever time it is. And if there's ever anything I can do, or if you just want someone to talk to—'

He went to bed anxious about her, determined if she rang again to insist that she should call the police; and resolved to call them himself if Ainger were crazy enough to come to his house and create a disturbance.

But it hadn't occurred to Robin Ainger to seek out Reynolds. That would draw unfavourable attention to himself, and, distraught as he was when he left the Rectory, he remained conscious of his cloth. It was not a moral consciousness, but rather an obsessive awareness of his clerical image. And so, although he drove away from Gillian in a rage, the sight of the church tower looming up at the end of St Botolph Street, dark against a starlit sky, reminded him almost immediately of his position in the community, and he slowed.

He had nothing in mind when he took out the car except the need to distance himself temporarily from Gillian. But as he drove, anger and self-pity began to give way gradually to unease. Had he perhaps made too much of what was, after all, a minor act of defiance on Gillian's part? Was he by any chance in danger of making himself look foolish?

It was twenty minutes to two when he garaged the car and let himself in to the Rectory. The hall light was still on, and Gillian came hurrying from the drawing-room in nightdress and dressing-gown, her hair hanging loose on her shoulders, her face apprehensive.

'Are you—is everything all right?'

He nodded, conscious chiefly of weariness and of the stiffness and soreness of his hand. He wanted to go to her, to put his arms round her and to be looked after, but he had been too much hurt to make so quick a reconciliation.

'Where have you been, Robin?' It was a nervous question, not an outraged demand, and he answered it with dignified melancholy.

'Just driving.'

Her apprehension vanished. She ran to him and put her hands on his chest, telling him how worried about him she had been. 'And, Robin, I shan't bother with those classes anymore. I've learned enough about technique to carry on with my sculpture at home, and that's what I'll do. It's stupid to let a hobby come between us.'

He drew a deep, victorious breath. 'I'm glad you see it that way. And now I must go to bed, I'm dog-tired and I'm taking an early service tomorrow. Did you get out the blankets for the spare bed?'

She blinked, and stepped back. 'I made it up, as a matter of fact,' she admitted, 'just in case... But surely, now—'

He saw the hurt in her face, and was not sorry. 'I'll sleep better on my own,' he said. 'I really am desperately tired.'

'Yes, I expect you are,' she agreed sadly. It seemed that giving up her classes and her friendship with Alec Reynolds was insufficient to restore her relationship with her husband, and she felt completely bereft; until she remembered that she had another friend.

'Just tell me this,' she begged. 'Janey Rolph, an Australian student I met in Yarchester, is coming to tea on Saturday. She's young and homesick, and I want her to feel that she's welcome here. You will be nice to her, won't you?'

Her husband felt that he could afford to be magnanimous. He bent his head and pressed his cheek for a moment against Gillian's hair.

'Don't worry, of course I'll be nice to her,' he said.

# Chapter 18

On her first visit, Janey Rolph parked her third-hand red Datsun, with the *Australia* sticker, just beyond the Rectory gates and on the opposite side of the road, under the copper beech trees that overhung the palings at the top of Parson's Close. Gillian, greeting her at the door, suggested that she should bring her car into the Rectory drive, but the girl declined.

'I'd rather leave it outside, thanks. Then I'll be ready for a quick getaway when you throw me out.'

'Why on earth should I want to do that?'

'You will, when I commit some desperate social blunder. This'll be the first time I've had tea with a clergyman's wife. If you hear an odd noise it'll be my knees knocking together.'

Gillian was disarmed. She was of course aware of the girl's striking looks: the urchin-cut fox-red hair, the full mouth, the large brown eyes. But nothing in Janey's nervous demeanour, or in Gillian's experience, suggested that the girl might be a potential rival. Far from feeling threatened by Janey's looks, Gillian felt flattered by them, as any plain woman does when an attractive one seeks her company.

Under the influence of tea and cherry buns, Janey seemed to relax. Gillian took her on a tour of the house, pleased to observe that the girl's hands went out with instinctive appreciation to touch the early nineteenth-century joinery. In the empty bedroom that Gillian used as a studio, Janey went straight to a completed plaster cast, the head of a young man, amateur in execution but boldly conceived. She stroked his profile with one finger.

'Hey, I like your friend,' she told Gillian. 'He's beaut.'

'Thank you. He was the first one I ever made, some years ago. Do you do anything like this?'

Janey pulled a wry face. 'No, I'm hopeless with my hands. I do envy your ability. I wish I had some kind of talent.'

'But you're an academic, a writer,' protested Gillian. 'What about your thesis?'

'*English Satirical Novelists, 1950 to 1980*? Dissecting their work's a destructive process, not a creative one.'

'Oh, but later on, when you've finished the thesis, you'll have more time to discover your own talents,' said Gillian with parson's-wife warmth and encouragement. 'Now, would you like to see the church? It really is rather fine. I expect we'll find my husband over there.'

It seemed a sensible precaution to introduce them in a place where Robin could be relied on to act with propriety. His behaviour, since the evening when Alec Reynolds came to supper, had been civil but cool, and Gillian was wary of him.

But Robin was in a good mood that evening. He was proud of St Botolph's, and enjoyed showing visitors round. And on Saturday evenings, when the urns were filled with fresh flowers and the organist, practising for the following day, was making a joyful noise unto the Lord, the church was always at its best.

His wife's friend was obviously impressed. Robin was

never to forget—although afterwards he did his best to obscure the memory by never willingly recalling it—his first sight of Janey Rolph. She was standing beside a pillar at the far end of the nave, small, fragile, her hair a glory against the grey stone, her face rapt as she gazed up at the angels that hovered under the lofty roof.

After he married, Robin had tried never to think of other women in physical terms. But what he permitted himself at that first meeting to see in Janey Rolph affected him far more deeply than any acknowledgement of her beauty. Gillian's bid for independence had hurt him so profoundly that he had regained a measure of stability during the past few days only by distancing himself from her. The realization that he was more dependent on her than she on him was terrifying. But Janey, lonely and vulnerable, was so obviously in need of care and protection that he responded to her immediately.

The girl was fascinated by everything he pointed out to her. The finest of the monumental brasses, that of Sir John Bedingfield and his lady, lying in the chancel almost as large as life, made her gasp with delight.

'Oh, but look—he's holding her hand!'

Sir John, who had died in 1410, was fully armoured from bascinet to spurs; except that he was not wearing his gauntlets. His bare right hand reached out to clasp that of Isabella his wife, who lay with her left hand on her breast and her eyes cast down, modest in plain gown and wimple. The dog at Sir John's feet looked up at them both with affectionate approval.

Janey crouched to touch the brass with reverent fingers. 'Oh, you're beaut,' she told the knight and his wife. 'You too, cobber,' she added to the dog.

She straightened slowly, still gazing at the engraving. 'It's like the Philip Larkin poem, *An Arundel Tomb*,' she said. 'I'd meant to go to Arundel, on a sort of pilgrimage. But now I've seen this, I don't need to.'

Gillian and Robin glanced at each other over the girl's head, and for the first time for what seemed like months they exchanged spontaneous smiles. Gillian's heart lifted, and she blessed Janey for having brought them together again. It seemed appropriate that at that moment the organ's sound swelled to a crescendo powerful enough to have kept the roof's angels afloat even if they had not been pegged into the hammer beams.

Michael Dade, the deputy organist—a good musician, and deputy only because he couldn't keep the choirboys in order—had seen Janey through his rear-view mirror and had expressed his admiration musically. When he finished playing he hurried round the pulpit so that he could meet her. He had sad brown eyes, lank dark hair that flopped over his beaky nose, and a bad stammer. On his organ bench he felt that he was someone of consequence, but by the time he faced Janey the musically aroused adrenalin had ebbed, leaving him shifting from foot to foot in a silent agony of embarrassment.

Gillian went to his rescue and introduced him to the girl. Janey expressed her admiration for his playing, and was patient and sympathetic when consonants eluded him. By the time she had finished chatting to him, both Gillian and Robin were impressed by her kindness. As for Michael Dade, he was already in love.

Janey made another conquest that evening. When she and Gillian returned to the Rectory, old Henry Bowers was just collecting his garden tools after weeding and staking the herbaceous plants that edged the drive. Janey was quick to admire his work and at supper—for which both Aingers insisted that she must stay—she talked with affection about her own grandfather. She listened when

Henry began to reminisce about Gallipoli, and encouraged him with questions; and the old man was so taken by her that he invited her with sly gallantry to call him Grandad. When she left eventually, seen off by all three of them, it was understood that she would be welcomed at the Rectory whenever she liked to call.

For the remainder of the evening, the Aingers talked Janey Rolph. They were captivated. She had told them that her student's permit to reside temporarily in the United Kingdom expired at the end of the academic year, and that she would have to leave the country in a few months' time, and this made them all the more anxious to see her as often as possible.

They were still talking Janey as they prepared for bed. Robin had been sleeping in the spare room ever since Alec Reynolds's visit, but having cleaned his teeth he wandered absent-mindedly in his pyjamas into the marital bedroom to continue the conversation.

'She was really bowled over by the brasses of Sir John and his wife, wasn't she? That poem she mentioned, *An Arundel Tomb*—what's it about?'

Gillian paused in the act of brushing her hair, and turned to look at her husband. 'Love,' she said. 'The enduring quality of love...'

It had been a long time. They hadn't made love for months, and even then—as in the previous two or three years—it had been nothing more than a perfunctory means of relieving physical tension, a hurried act that had left them both feeling besmirched. But now it was beautiful, a long slow exchange of tenderness and mutual adoration that left them exhausted with joy.

It was only then, lying peacefully in her husband's arms, that Gillian admitted to herself how unhappy she had been, and for how long. She had never stopped loving

Robin, she knew that, but it was many years since she had been able to like him. This evening, though, he was quite different from the overbearing, bitingly sarcastic man she had reluctantly become accustomed to living with. He seemed his old self again, the Robin she had fallen in love with sixteen years before.

It was weeks before she made the connection, in anything but the most general terms, between the resumption of their sex life and the first meeting between Robin and Janey Rolph. And when she did make the connection, the hurt of it was that she knew she would never know, despite his protestations, which one of them had been in Robin's mind when he was making love to her.

# Chapter 19

There was no need for Janey Rolph to wait until she had finished her thesis before taking stock of her other talents. Her major talent was for manipulating people, and she had been exercising it for years.

She needed people; fed on them. She could never bear to live alone, but she was incapable of sustaining a long-term relationship with any one person. Instead, she cultivated childless married couples.

What she had in mind, when she sought the company of married women, was their friendship and their hospitality. She was a perpetual student, moving from one university to another in search of degrees and diplomas, and she was perpetually short of money. If she played her hand properly, she could be sure that sooner or later her new friends would take pity on her 'homesickness' for the town she hoped never to see again, and would invite her to move in with them.

Janey made a delightful house-guest: amusing, considerate, endearingly anxious to make no social blunders, to cause no trouble, to be treated as one of the family. She had a good eye for picking out unworldly people as potential hosts, and before long her welfare and happiness would become their prime consideration. They would plan meals round her likes and dislikes, and rearrange or miss appointments so that they could take her on sightseeing expeditions. Like a cuckoo in the nest, she would gradually take over their lives.

But the material benefits that Janey obtained were incidental. The people themselves were her real interest. She listened, and she watched, and she encouraged separate confidences from husband and wife, and before long she knew all their hopes and dreams and fears, their strengths, their weaknesses, and the current state of their marriage.

It was possession of this kind of knowledge that Janey prized above all else. The sense of power that it conferred on her, the puppet-master's authority, gave her a far greater kick than she could have obtained from drugs or alcohol. She made no immediate plans to use her power but sooner or later, in every friendship, she would find the temptation irresistible. It was almost inevitable that by the time she was ready to move on, the marriage would have foundered. Janey felt no compunction because she felt no responsibility; she had observed, as a child, that marriage was anyway a process of mutual destruction.

'She's widened our horizons so much,' said Gillian Ainger to her husband on the night when Janey moved into the Rectory. They had just gone to bed, having made sure that their guest was comfortably settled, and Gillian was smiling with self-congratulation in the dark. Janey was exactly what she and Robin had needed, someone from outside the parish to talk to, someone with completely different ideas and interests. 'She's really enriched our lives, hasn't she?'

'She's certainly done that,' agreed Robin. 'Your

father's, too. He'd have made a good grandfather, wouldn't he? Pity we couldn't have given him some grandchildren.'

'We did try.'

'And we're still trying.'

Later, from across the corridor, Janey heard Gillian's prolonged orgasmic cry. Listened for it, identified it, and, with neither envy nor malice, recorded it on her mental retrieval system for possible future use.

The only person who was capable of making Janey uneasy was Athol Garrity. She couldn't believe that anyone with the power which his knowledge of her background gave him would be uninterested in using it.

The Aingers' invitation to move into the Rectory had provided her with the excuse she needed to shake him off without running the risk of offending him. She had lied to him about where she was going, and she was disturbed and angry when, one afternoon early in June, she found him in St Botolph Street beside her car. He was sitting on the ground with his back to the palings that fenced Parson's Close, his big hands, resting on his bony knees, cradling a beer-can. On his left hand he wore a conspicuous silver knuckle-duster ring that he had acquired while he was backpacking round the eastern Mediterranean.

'What the hell are you doing here?' demanded Janey.

'Just came to look you up.' He grinned at her with wry admiration, showing a mouthful of excellent teeth in his long jaw. 'Got the right address from the university registry. You always were a soddin' liar, Janey Rolph.'

She tried to persuade him to go away, but a man he had met in a nearby pub had told him that there was money to be made by brass-rubbing. Garrity had immediately gone prospecting in the church, where he had met the Rector and acquired the offer of a pitch for his tent, and an invitation to supper at the Rectory.

Janey was quietly furious. But then she remembered that Gillian Ainger had already had beer spilled over her by Athol; with luck, Gillian would soon discourage him. And if not, Janey reflected, she would have to find some other way of getting rid of him.

The Aingers dated the start of their troubles from Athol Garrity's arrival in Breckham Market. Everything had been fine, they told each other, until Athol appeared.

Janey had secured such a hold upon their affections that they ignored the fact that their rediscovered marital happiness began to deteriorate almost as soon as she moved in with them. The ease and relaxation that they experienced at first in her company had been replaced by a new tension. It was as if she had ushered them on to a pleasantly slow-moving conveyor belt that had almost immediately speeded up and was now whizzing them, helpless, through their own lives.

The strain and bewilderment showed on both their faces. They tried to carry on as usual with their duties in the church and the community, but Gillian was almost invariably late for her appointments and Robin lost his concentration. Neither of them could any longer be relied on to remember the messages they were given; or the things they promised to do; except where Janey was involved. Unable—or unwilling—to identify her as the source of their turmoil, they focused their resentment on Athol Garrity.

Robin felt, angrily, that Athol had conned him. Their

initial conversation in the church had given him the impression that the Australian was genuinely interested in church brasses. And when he learned that Garrity had come to Breckham to seek out Janey because he was one of her childhood friends, he had welcomed him in the hope of pleasing her.

His gut reaction, when he saw them together, took him completely by surprise. Janey's indifference to her fellow-countryman was clear, but Garrity's familiarity with her, and the way his eyes followed her about, made Robin's stomach muscles tighten sickeningly. He longed to get rid of him, but he was unable to say so either to Gillian or to Janey because that might advertise his jealousy.

Old Henry Bowers also wanted to see the back of the man. Garrity copied Janey in calling him Grandad, but without a by-your-leave; and he wasn't in the least interested in Gallipoli. Besides, Henry could see that his daughter disliked Garrity, and he hated to see her upset. For the first time in his life, the old man's anecdotal references to bloody Aussies carried an undertone of malice.

As for Gillian, she found it difficult to revise her initial opinion of Garrity, despite the fact that he arrived at the Rectory sober and made a painstaking, if imperfect, attempt to weed the obscenities out of his vocabulary. Janey encouraged her in her dislike, and Gillian made it clear to her friend that she had no intention of inviting him a second time.

But that was before she saw the look that her husband gave the man.

The shock of it, of seeing the narrow glitter of jealousy in Robin's eyes when Garrity put a large, silver-ringed hand casually on Janey's waist, left Gillian strangely lightheaded. She couldn't believe what she had seen because she didn't want to believe it. Other married men might well become infatuated with a girl as attractive as Janey, but surely not Robin? As she had cause to know, he put a strictly literal interpretation on their marriage vows.

But whatever was going on in Robin's head, Gillian was unwilling to blame Janey. The girl had always treated him as an older brother, someone she admired and respected. She had never tried, as hapless women parishioners sometimes did, to contrive opportunities to be alone with him.

Even so, Gillian did some rapid thinking. If Robin really was hankering after Janey, the most sensible and civilized way to deal with the situation would be to encourage more unattached men of the girl's own age to come to the Rectory. With luck, she might fall for one of them; and if she didn't, their youthful presence should help Robin to put his feelings in perspective during the few remaining weeks of Janey's visit.

Meanwhile, Athol Garrity was better than no one. Gillian invited him to come again. She also invited Michael Dade, the deputy organist, two young teachers, and Martin Tait, the police detective sergeant who had recently investigated the theft of some church silver.

'What are you trying to do?' Janey protested, laughing. 'Marry me off, or something?'

'Why not?' said Gillian, trying to extend the laughter. 'You've always said that you don't like Australian men, so it's high time you met some unattached English ones.'

Janey became thoughtful. 'You know, if I were to marry an Englishman, I could stay over here at the end of July instead of having to leave the country.' She smiled at Gillian, her voice teasing, her eyes as always shrewdly calculating the effect of her words. 'How would it be if I settled permanently in Breckham Market?'

'Lovely!' said Gillian, without daring to wonder why the prospect made her heart founder.

But Janey had no intention of settling in the town, and the young men were a nuisance. She ignored Michael Dade and Martin Tait and the teachers, and she got rid of Athol Garrity by the simple expedient of encouraging him to make a rubbing of the Bedingfield brass in St Botolph's. She advised him on the purchase of the equipment, and she set it out for him in the chancel, using the great Bible and piles of prayer books to hold down the paper. To refresh him during his work, she put a few cans of beer on the altar; to keep him entertained, she provided her transistor radio. Just before she slipped out through the vestry door, she turned up the radio volume to its fullest extent. Then she left him to face the verger's anguish and the Rector's wrath.

As she hoped, Robin forbade Athol to enter either the church or the Rectory again. Janey was to see no more of her fellow-countryman for three weeks, until 29 July. She guessed that he had gone to London, and she took note of the fact that he had left his tent pitched in Parson's Close. It was small, but it would be adequate for her purpose.

# Chapter 20

Alec Reynolds often thought of Gillian during the course of the summer, and wondered how things were between her and her husband. One Saturday afternoon in mid-July he drove over to Breckham Market and sat in his car in St Botolph Street, in the hope of seeing her. His image of her had been that of a younger version of his late wife, but in good health. The thinner, anxiety-ridden appearance of the woman who eventually hurried out of the Rectory gate, carrying a shopping-basket, shocked him.

They exchanged face-saving untruths: Gillian was fine; Reynolds had come to Breckham primarily on business. He invited her to have tea with him in a café, but she refused. She made the light excuse that it might give rise to gossip in the town, but what really worried her was that Robin was in his study pretending to write tomorrow's sermon, and Janey was in her room finishing her thesis. She was reluctant to leave the two of them alone in the house for longer than she had to.

The strain of it all, of trying to continue with her work in the parish while her own emotions were in a state of turmoil, was wearing Gillian down. Her hands often shook, and she could hear her voice growing shrill. The only thing that kept her going was the thought that after the end of July her life would return to normal.

Meanwhile, Alec Reynolds was a welcome link with normality, and she accepted a lift as far as the shoppers' car park.

'How are things?' he asked as he drove. 'Truthfully?' She closed her eyes. She had never been a woman who cried easily—parsons' wives are not expected to be emotional, and Gillian wasn't—but she was so tense that the unexpected gentleness of his words brought tears prickling up behind her eyelids. She held them back, but told him how abominable Athol Garrity had been; and added that it was a strain to have an unattached girl as a long-term guest, however pleasant she was and however much she understood the importance of keeping a low profile to minimize parish gossip.

'It isn't gossip that's the problem, though, is it?' said Reynolds. He had seen Janey Rolph in the pub in Yarchester, he knew how very attractive she was, and he could guess why Gillian was distressed. He braked vigorously to a stop in the car park. 'Tell the girl to pack her bags and go.'

'But it isn't her fault that Robin's infatuated by her. Besides, he won't do anything about it. He's a priest. He's convinced of the sanctity of marriage.'

Reynolds snorted. He took off his glasses and polished them with a cloth that he kept with a spare pair of glasses in a case under the dash.

'Don't be ingenuous, Gillian. Priest, doctor, lawyer— what does his profession matter? He's a man.'

She rounded on him angrily. 'And are all men by definition lechers? That's a cynical suggestion of the kind I might expect from some of our parishioners, but not from you, Alec. I'd have thought you might acknowledge the finer feelings. There are such things as trust and fidelity, you know.'

Reynolds, who had been unswervingly faithful to his wife, was hurt and annoyed. 'Yes, I do know. But your husband is a man who is ruled by his emotions. Didn't he suspect you of having an affair with me?'

'All the more reason why I shouldn't misinterpret his friendship with Janey,' insisted Gillian. 'Don't you see, that's exactly what the gossips would do? It's what I hate so much about parish life, and I won't be a party to it. All right, I'm worried about Robin's infatuation, but I know it's no more than that. I *trust* him.'

❈ ❈ ❈

She was sorry to quarrel with Alec Reynolds, but having reasserted her faith in her husband she returned home in due course with a full shopping-basket and a lighter heart. When Robin came to look for her in the kitchen, she greeted him almost gaily, offering him tea.

She was answered by a breathy silence. He stood in the doorway staring over her head. His eyeballs were as dark as the whites of eggs that have been hard-boiled but not plunged immediately into cold water, and his face was ugly.

'I don't want any tea,' he said in a slow, strangled voice. 'I don't think I want anything from you ever again. You've lied to me and you've cheated me. You let me think that you'd given up seeing that man Reynolds, but you've obviously kept in touch with him all the time.'

'But I—'

'Don't try to deny it. I saw you, getting into his car and driving off. Where have you been? What have you been doing?'

She tried to explain, but Robin insisted that she was deceiving him. When she told him that all she was concerned about—all she had talked about with Reynolds—

was their relationship as husband and wife, Robin's eyes glittered with rage.

'How dare you?' His voice dropped into a register so low that she had never heard it from him before. 'How *dare* you talk to anyone about me, as though I were a piece of public property? I'm not public property, I'm a person, I'm a private person, and I have a right to my own private life—'

'But I didn't—'

He struck his fist on the kitchen table. 'Don't *lie* to me! Don't lie to me anymore, you've done enough lying, you've done enough—'

He began to cry. Sobs of rage and frustration came wrenching up out of his chest as he sank into a chair and began to beat his hand against the kitchen table. Aghast, Gillian went to him and nervously touched his shoulder. 'Robin—Robin dear—'

He flung her off. His teeth were grinding together. 'Get away! Get away from me! I *hate* you!'

She backed, terrified. He was ill, he was out of his mind, she must telephone the doctor—

And then she saw that Janey was standing in the doorway, watching.

'He's ill—ill—' Gillian stammered. 'I'll just go—'

The girl understood. 'You go and get the doctor. I'll keep an eye on him,' she said.

Gillian ran from the kitchen. Robin had stopped beating the table and was now sitting sprawled across it, his head on his arms, his shoulders heaving.

Janey reached out a hand and stroked his wavy hair. 'It'll be all right, Rob,' she murmured. 'Don't worry, everything'll be all right.'

He lifted his head, turned to her, put his arms round her and began to shiver and cry quietly on her breast.

Months afterwards, Gillian decided that she herself had been responsible for starting the affair between her husband and Janey, in the sense that she was the one who had invited the girl into their home. She had to learn to live with the fact that all the subsequent happenings— passion and hatred, tragedy and death, fear and lying, waste and mourning—stemmed from her own obstinate determination to go against her husband's wishes and look for friends outside the parish. As the repercussions spread, she found herself thinking again and again, sometimes in panic, sometimes in lamentation, 'If only...'

If only she had tried to comfort Robin herself that afternoon; but she hadn't enough passion in her make-up, or compassion either. And then, the build-up of tension between them had been so great that it could be dispelled only by catharsis.

If only she had telephoned the doctor; but that would have added to her husband's rage. He would never have forgiven her if she had let the doctor see him in a state of emotional and mental turmoil.

She peered nervously into the kitchen. Robin was sitting with one elbow on the table, his head propped by his hand, occasionally giving a small sob. His other arm was extended limply across the table. Janey, sitting beside him, was holding his hand consolingly in hers. She made no attempt to move when Gillian reappeared, and it did not occur to the older woman that there was anything other than helpfulness and friendship in the posture. They whispered to each other, agreeing that as Robin was calmer it would be a good idea if Gillian went out for a breath of fresh air while Janey continued to sit with him.

If only...

Gillian crossed St Botolph Street and walked under the dark summer canopy of the copper beech trees, into the sunlit quiet of Parson's Close. She was deeply shocked and completely bewildered by her husband's behaviour. It didn't occur to her until later that his outburst of hatred was both an expression of his struggle to suppress his feelings for Janey and an attempt to justify those feelings. All she could think of at the time was the injustice of his allegations against her, and her growing fear for his sanity. She was almost afraid to go back to the house.

And yet she must go back, if only to make substitution arrangements for the following day's services. Appearances must be kept up; the parish routine must be maintained, even though Robin was ill. She concentrated on the details she would have to attend to, feeling better for the mental activity. As for Robin—thank God Janey was there to keep an eye on him.

But Robin, despite his turmoil, had also thought of the church. Detaching himself from Janey's hand, he had stumbled out of the Rectory and sought refuge in St Botolph's. For once, it was empty. The verger would be back at dusk to lock up, but for the next hour Robin had the shadow-filled grandeur of the church to himself.

He sank to his knees in his stall behind the lectern and put his head in his hands. Prayer was impossible; he had lost communication with God months, if not years, ago. But here, in a place where prayer had been valid for five centuries, he might at least be able to dispel some of the black thoughts that seethed in his mind.

He sensed rather than saw Janey enter the church. The clunk of the iron latch as the door was closed, and the grating sound as the massive key was turned in the lock, failed to disturb him, but all his senses were so attuned to her that he knew she was there, walking quietly down the aisle towards him. He knew exactly how she looked, her face gravely intent, her hair a living glory against the pillars of carved stone.

She passed him, walking on up the chancel. He opened his fingers and looked through them. She rolled back the carpet immediately below the altar steps, and stood gazing down at the Bedingfield brass. Without thought or volition he rose from his knees and walked up the chancel towards her.

Neither of them spoke. Robin was aware of nothing but Janey as they stood stiffly side by side, in much the same attitude as the knight and his lady at their feet. It seemed not only natural but inevitable that as they stood there Janey's hand should move into his.

He felt their flesh jolt together, as though welded by an electric current. Slowly, he turned his head towards her. His ears were filled with the thunder of his blood, and the world had contracted to the size and shape of her lips. His own were dry. He heard himself croak a faint, token protest: 'Not here—'

But Janey, guiding him towards the rolled-up carpet, said, 'Where better? Sir John and Isabella will understand.'

# Chapter 21

What affected Gillian most, when Robin told her that he loved Janey, that he had made love to her, and that he intended to go on doing so as long as she remained in England, was the blow to her self-esteem. She didn't blame Robin for what had happened, or Janey, but she blamed herself for letting it happen.

Superficially, life at the Rectory and in the parish went on much as usual for the next eight days. Robin insisted that he wasn't ill. He refused to see the doctor, and said that he intended to go on working. Gillian tried at first to reason with him, to point out that he couldn't preach and lead prayers, let alone administer the sacraments, at the same time as he was committing adultery; but she was unable to get through to him. Robin moved through each day's work like a zombie. His congregation, thinking how ill he looked, attributed his mistakes and strange pauses in church to physical pain, and did what they could to lighten his burdens.

At home, Robin and Gillian spoke little to each other. He moved out of their bedroom into the spare room lately occupied by Janey, who in Athol Garrity's absence had taken over his tent. Gillian was aware of Robin's nocturnal excursions only if she heard the floorboards creak or his door open and close. Her instinct was to walk out on him, at least temporarily, but as the conscientious wife of a parson her priorities were clear to her: she covered for him, kept him going, held the affairs of the parish together. Sometimes, exhausted, she would only shrug and mutter that it wouldn't be for long.

He would have found it easier if she had shouted at him. He knew that he was behaving insupportably, and he longed to have an opportunity to shout back at her. He felt that, in snatching a few days' happiness with Janey, he was for the first time in his life doing what he himself wanted to do, instead of what others expected of him. The pressures of clerical life, and the public's insistence on a blameless clerical lifestyle, had become more than he could sustain. *I'm not just a parson*, he wanted to shout at his wife and the world, *I'm a person. What about what I want, for a change?*

But his wife gave him no excuse to shout at her, and he could never shout at the world because his sense of guilt was too strong. Not that he felt sinful; he was too far out of touch with God for that. His guilt came from the knowledge that if his conduct were made public he would lose his job, his home, and possibly his wife. And he wanted desperately to keep all three.

The hostility that he had expected from Gillian came instead from her father. The Aingers tried to conceal what was happening from Henry Bowers, but the old man was no fool. He had always despised his son-in-law, and now he had cause to hate him.

'Why you dirty bastard,' he roared, when full realization came to him. He advanced on Robin, his eyebrows ferocious, his great gnarled hands shaking with fury. 'I'll strangle you with my bare hands, I'll—'

Robin backed rapidly out of the room, and Gillian pulled her father away. 'Stop it, Dad! I won't have you making threats.' The old man stood panting and swearing. 'Who does he bloody think he is, to treat my daughter like this? A parson? I'll give him bloody parson—'

'No you won't,' said Gillian wearily. 'Listen to me, Dad. Sit down and listen. I need your help.'

He had begun to chunter about Janey. 'That little gal, eh? And I treated her like me own grand-daughter...and all the time she's nothing but a tart!' He thumped his fist on the arm of his chair. 'Bloody Aussies—nothing but trouble. By God, if ever she comes back to this house I'll—'

Gillian seized his shoulders and shook him. 'Stop it, do you hear? Robin's not himself, he's ill. He'll get over it as soon as Janey goes, but we *must* keep this to ourselves. You mustn't breathe a word of what has happened to anyone, or Robin will be ruined. And if that happens, it won't just be Robin who suffers, it'll be me as well. Do you understand? So promise me this: you won't talk about us in the town, ever, and you won't say or do anything to hurt Robin—or Janey either, come to that. Say that you promise, Dad?'

The old man shuffled and sulked, but he loved his daughter too much to refuse her anything.

Janey Rolph was bored.

In four days' time, on Tuesday, 31 July, she would be flying to the United States. She had her visa and her airline ticket. England held no further interest for her. She had seen what she wanted to see, had disrupted a stable relationship between two post-graduate students in Yarchester, and completed her thesis demolishing the literary reputation of three contemporary novelists. Her major achievement had been to induce the Rector of Breckham Market to make love to her in his own church, but for once her timing had gone awry. The passionate kiss and its consummation should have been postponed until the eve of her departure. Anything after it was bound to be an anti-climax.

Robin now spent most of his time with her agonizing tediously, over drinks and meals in country pubs, about what he was doing to Gillian. He was still fervent in his lovemaking, but Janey was not particularly interested in sex and she found that the novelty of having it in church soon wore off. The vestry was uncomfortable. So was Athol Garrity's tent. She decided that she would prefer to spend her last weekend in England in comfort, and to give Gillian—who had showed such bovine confidence in the stability of her marriage—the experience of lying in bed alone and listening to her enjoyment.

She announced her decision to Robin late in the evening of Friday, 27 July, reducing him to impotence by the enormity of her demand. He returned home earlier than usual. Gillian's light was still on, and he knocked on the door of their bedroom before venturing in and delivering Janey's message. It would only be for three days, he pleaded…no, of course he wouldn't share the spare room with Janey, he'd put up a camp-bed in one of the empty bedrooms…yes, of course he saw Gillian's point of view. 'Or would you rather go away for the weekend?' he finished desperately. ('And if she doesn't like it, she needn't stay,' Janey had told him.)

Gillian stared at him, her eyes hot with misery. 'Is that what you want me to do?'

'No. Yes, if you like. I don't know.' He put his head in his hands, exhausted by worry and guilt and emotion. He had thought that Janey was fragile, in need of his help and protection, but tonight he had seen a new side of her nature, a strength that drained him completely. 'She— she's making threats.'

He explained, haltingly, what Janey had done. They had gone out for the evening in her red Datsun and on the way, having earlier telephoned him at work to arrange it, she had picked up Michael Dade. During the course of the evening she had made amorous advances to the lovesick church organist, encouraging him to think that she would be willing to marry him. Robin had seethed with silent jealousy. But after she had packed Michael off home, Janey had explained that marriage to him would simply be a means of staying in Breckham Market, so as to be near Robin.

'And I couldn't bear it,' he told his wife. He sat on the edge of her bed, sweating with fear. His stomach was churning, as it always did when he was afraid, and his breath was foul. 'I couldn't have her living in Breckham with someone else, gazing at me with those great eyes, tormenting me... I begged her not to marry him, and she said she wouldn't if we'd take her back into the house.'

'Of course she wouldn't marry Michael,' said Gillian. 'What a cruel thing to let him think!'

'But she might!' He shivered. 'You don't know her— she might do anything. And I can't take the risk. I daren't. Just let her stay in the house for this weekend, to keep her quiet, *please.*'

But Gillian had reached her sticking-point. She had been humiliated enough.

'No,' she said slowly, 'I'm damned if I will.'

Her sense of humiliation had prevented Gillian from telephoning Alec Reynolds before, but she did so next morning, apologizing for having quarrelled with him over his assessment of her husband's character.

Reynolds took no pleasure from the fact that he had been right about Robin Ainger. He liked Gillian too much for that. It was a Saturday, and he would have driven straight to Breckham Market to give her what support he could—Ainger was in no position to raise any objection now—but he was about to set off for London and a weekend with his woman friend.

He delayed long enough to listen carefully to Gillian. She asked his advice, and he gave it. Never mind about the parish for a moment, he told her; think of yourself. Until recently you were not at all happy with your husband, and now he's broken the trust you put in him. Do you still want to remain his wife?

For a few moments Gillian said nothing. Then she answered in a strangled voice, 'I suppose I'm a fool, but yes, I do. I still love the wretched man, you see. Whatever he does, I'll stay loyal to him.'

'All right, then, my dear,' said Reynolds, half envious of him, half exasperated with her. 'If that's what you want, then you must stay put in your own home. Don't let that girl drive you out, or give way to her blackmail. And stay calm, because your husband's obviously got himself into a mess, and he's going to need all your strength and sanity to help him out of it. Good luck, Gillian. I'll call and see you tomorrow evening on my way back from London.'

On the last Saturday in July, St Botolph's church was busy with weddings. Gillian steered her husband through the long day. When he had heard the third couple make their vows, and had sent them off with his blessing, he returned to the Rectory to change into casual clothes. Then he set off in the evening sunlight to meet Janey.

Gillian watched him leave, hoping that he would do as she had suggested and find a hotel where the girl could spend the weekend. She knew that he had taken his toothbrush and razor with him, and she assumed that she would not see him again before early service the next day. But Robin was careful never to take Janey out in his own car, which was well known in Breckham Market. They always used the Datsun. Janey insisted on driving, and so she controlled the length of their journeys, and their destination.

Robin was back at the Rectory shortly after nine o'clock twitching with panic.

'We went to a hotel for a meal, but she refused to stay. She says she intends to sleep here. She's just gone to collect her things from the tent, and then she's coming.'

Gillian had tried to go on staying calm, as Alec Reynolds had advised, but this was too much. Anger began to mount inside her, rising up in a red tide that made her feel ready to do battle with anyone; and to hell with being a parson's wife.

'Oh no she's bloody well not,' she said.

She ran round the house, locking doors and closing windows. Robin hurried after her, protesting. 'But you can't keep her out! You don't know what she'll do!'

'She won't marry Michael Dade, I'm quite sure of that.'

'She's not talking about that anymore. But she says if we don't let her in, she'll make trouble. She'll wake the neighbours, smash windows—'

'You know perfectly well we haven't any neighbours. And if she dares to do any damage, I'll send for the police.'

'But then everything will come out! Everyone will know what's been happening! My whole career—our whole life—will be ruined. It's not that I want her here, I swear it. I'm trying to protect you, surely you can see that?'

She saw the sweat on his face, and smelled fear on his breath. 'Having your mistress in my house isn't the kind of protection I want, Robin,' she said. 'If you're really concerned about our life together—if you really don't want her here—then you must send her away.'

'But I can't...she's too strong for me! Oh Gillian, please—' For the first time since his affair with Janey began, he looked his wife in the eyes. 'I can't fight her alone. For the love of God, help me.'

# Chapter 22

They stood together at the top of the stairs listening to the ringing of the front-door bell, and then to the knocking at the side door, and at the back. There was a silence for ten minutes, and then the telephone began to ring. When Gillian answered it, the line went dead. After four such calls, she left the receiver off.

The assault on the doors started again half an hour later, with increased intensity. Handles were tried. Flung gravel rattled against the windows. Robin and Gillian, emerging from their separate bedrooms to meet in the upstairs corridor, found themselves clutching at each other in mutual alarm.

It was Henry Bowers who, unprompted, resolved the situation. Exasperated by the disturbance, he pushed up the sash window of his bedroom and bellowed into the warm night air, 'Be off with you, you noisy trollop, or I'll come down and shut you up meself!'

To the Aingers' surprise and relief, Janey went.

Robin's Sunday was, as always, fully occupied, and Gillian accompanied him to all the morning services. Janey's Datsun disappeared from St Botolph Street during the course of the morning, and Gillian began to think that they had won a victory.

They were about to set off for Evensong when Alec Reynolds arrived on his way back from London, looking so drawn and ill that Robin agreed that Gillian must stay and listen to him. She offered him coffee, but all he needed was a glass. He produced a half-bottle of whisky from his pocket, poured himself a large double, and told Gillian that Lesley had decided to marry a man she had met in London; the weekend had been their last together. Her announcement had taken him completely by surprise. He felt, he said, that his life had now completely fallen apart. Nothing seemed to matter anymore.

Gillian said what she could to console and encourage him. He was on his third whisky, and obviously unfit to drive, so she persuaded him to stay for a meal. She expected Robin back for supper by seven-thirty, but when he didn't appear by eight, she and her father and Reynolds ate without him.

It was nearly nine o'clock before Robin came back, in a state near to collapse. Janey had attended Evensong, walking up the aisle just as the service was about to begin, her hair lighting the gloom. She had sat in a front pew, where all the congregation could see her, and there had been whisperings and nudgings and murmurings of speculation when Robin panicked, stammered, and dried up. And after he had somehow stumbled his way through, she had met him outside the church, whisked him away in her car, and given him an ultimatum.

The congregation had now seen her, she said. During the course of the day she had made it her business to find out who the verger was, and the churchwardens, and the members of the parochial church council. If she wasn't taken back into the Rectory, she intended to call on them at their homes that evening and tell them that Robin had taken advantage of her loneliness in a foreign country and had seduced her in the church.

Gillian drew a deep breath. 'Where is she now?'

'In the drive, waiting for me to fetch her. And this time she won't go away. We *must* take her in, Gillian, or we'll be finished.'

She walked out of the front door. Robin sat huddled at the foot of the stairs, his head in his hands. Henry Bowers and Alec Reynolds, who had both overheard Robin's story, stood in the hall listening shamelessly to what was going on in the drive.

The sun had gone down and dusk was gathering. The old man's roses and peonies and gladioli had closed their petals for the night, and Janey's hair was the brightest thing in the garden. She leaned gracefully against the inner side of the closed gate, waiting with confidence to be invited into the house.

Gillian paused when she was still some yards from the girl and spoke to her loudly and clearly. 'It's no good, Janey. You can't blackmail us like this. You see, it's been tried before.' She knew that her voice was unsteady, but she plunged on. 'It's a sad fact that some women fantasize about their relationship with clergymen. It's one of the recognized hazards of clerical life, particularly when the man is as good-looking as Robin.'

That was true. He had always, throughout his career, had an accompanying flotilla of admiring women parishioners. He was normally adept at fending them off, but one or two, more persistent or less well balanced than the others, had tried to manoeuvre him into compromising situations and then, disappointed, had spread their fantasies throughout the parish. It had been a great embarrassment for him, although Gillian had always felt more keenly for the unhappy women; but then, no one had ever taken their allegations seriously. Gillian knew that if Janey spoke out her story would be totally credible, but she stood her ground and denied it.

'So no one would believe you. They know Robin's views on the sanctity of marriage, and they'd assume that you were upset because he'd rejected you. They'd think you were a silly, hysterical girl who was trying to take her revenge.'

Janey's stance had altered from graceful to taut. She started to say something, but she was interrupted by a cheerful shout of greeting from across the road. Athol Garrity, full of beer after his visit to the Concorde on his return from London, had flopped out for an hour in his tent before emerging from Parson's Close to see whether he could find her. After a moment's hesitation, Janey went out to talk to him. Gillian remained where she was. Her father and Alec Reynolds, both admiring her courage, walked out into the driveway and stood behind her. Robin, hardly daring to believe that her bluff would work, followed them.

Presently Janey returned to the gate. 'All right,' she said, looking at the four who now faced her, her voice hard with contempt. 'I don't care a toss one way or the other—I'm off to spend my last two nights in London, anyway. Breckham Market's the most boring place in this pathetic little country, and I'm tired of you whingeing Poms. But listen to this: perhaps people wouldn't believe *me* if I told them about Robin, but they'll believe Athol. They'll know he's got no reason to invent things. And they've all seen me in church, remember, they've seen Robin stutter and lose his nerve because I was there. So I've told Athol what to do, and he's promised to make a start first thing in the morning, as soon as he's slept the beer off. He's a good mate, Athol, and he'll do anything to please me. He'll drop you in it right up to your Pommy necks!'

She slammed the Rectory gate, kissed Athol Garrity good-bye, climbed into her red Datsun, and went. Garrity stood waving amiably after her, and then wandered back across St Botolph Street towards the gate that led into Parson's Close.

Drunk or sober, he knew Janey too well to agree to become involved in one of her feuds; knowing him equally well, she had not even asked. Her lie about her conversation with Athol was simply a parting exercise of power. She calculated that, in their emotional distress, her hearers would believe her implicitly. And they did.

The time was nine-thirty-two, the date was 29 July. Of the four people who stood in the Rectory drive and watched Garrity cross the road, three would never see him alive again.

# Part 3—This Spring

# Chapter 23

For the best part of a month after Athol Garrity's remains were buried, Chief Inspector Quantrill kept a discreet eye on the activities of the Rector and his wife. He observed that their tensions seemed to increase rather than diminish with the passage of time, but he learned nothing new about them. Old Henry Bowers made no more excursions to the Boot, so there was no opportunity for conversation with him. Regretfully, Quantrill began to put Garrity's death out of his mind; he had crimes enough to investigate, without inventing others.

On Monday, 3 April, a morning of bright sun after a wet weekend, he was forty miles away from Breckham investigating a country-house burglary. It was Detective Constable Ian Wigby, minding the office, who took the telephone message that the body of a man had been found by a security guard behind one of the many empty factories on the industrial estate. Wigby radioed the news to the Chief Inspector, received instructions, and was on the scene within ten minutes. By the time Quantrill arrived, the police surgeon had certified the man dead, the photographer was making a record of the area, and the divisional scene-of-crime officer was measuring and marking off the footprints that had been left round the body on the damp sandy ground.

There was no doubt about the dead man's identity. Wigby knew him well; they were both regulars at the Boot. 'One of the Bedingfields,' he reported. 'Kevin, Reggie's youngest. Died some time yesterday, the Doc estimates, probably as a result of cracking his head open when he fell. He certainly went a cropper.'

Kevin Bedingfield's body—rain-sodden, open-eyed, open-mouthed—was lying sprawled on its back, the head on some of the broken bricks that lay scattered on the waste ground behind the abandoned factory. He was a young man, not much more than twenty, swarthy and well built. The bricks beneath his dark wet head, and the weeds and the sandy earth below the bricks, were rusted with trickles of blood.

'Dr Thomson thinks there's a bruise on the side of the jaw that could be consistent with a heavy blow,' went on Wigby, 'but he's not committing himself.'

'Understandably,' said Quantrill, knowing the police surgeon's reluctance to trespass on pathologists' territory, 'but we'll know for sure after the post-mortem. How does it look to you, Keith?'

'Beautiful,' said the young civilian scene-of-crime officer. He was too short to join the force but full of compensatory, blinkered enthusiasm for his specialized work. 'The footprints couldn't be clearer. Eliminating the victim's and the security guard's, there's just one set. The man you want to interview wears leather size tens, so he's tall, and as the prints aren't deep he's probably thin-to-medium in build. It looks as though he and the victim arrived here separately, and then had a short scuffle.'

'During which it would seem that he knocked Kevin down...and that's odd,' said Quantrill. 'The boy's big enough to have held his own, and the Bedingfields are a tough family.'

Wigby shook his head. 'Kevin's always been a bit of a softy. He's been in trouble, like the rest of the family, but he's gone straight for the past couple of years, poor sod.' The phrase was careless, almost callous, but it was Wigby's way of expressing compassion for a fellow drinker and darts player. 'He wouldn't have gone out looking for aggro, I'm sure of that. He got married last September, and he's been full of talk about the baby his wife's expecting.'

'This'll go extra hard with her, then,' said Quantrill. He heard a car stop at the front of the building and saw that it contained his colleague from the county scene-of-crime squad. 'I want to know everything you can tell me about Kevin Bedingfield, Ian, but we can talk later over a bite to eat. I'll brief Inspector Colman now, while you go and tell Kevin's family and see if you can find out what he was up to when he came here.'

'Reggie Bedingfield cried when I told him,' said Wigby. 'Sentimental old git. Considering the number of times we've done him for assault... Mind you, I found him in the Jolly Butchers, so I reckon his tears were all of 83 degrees proof.'

He looked unappreciatively at his cup of canteen coffee. He had anticipated that the Chief Inspector would buy him a pie and a pint while they talked in the comfort of a pub, but Quantrill, whose wife had sent him out that morning with a packet of crusty ham sandwiches to sustain him during his investigation of the country-house burglary, had elected to economize by lunching off them in his office.

'So what did you find out from Reggie?' Quantrill asked.

'Nothing useful. But his wife's tougher, and she talked. The baby's arrived, by the way—their umpteenth grandchild. Kevin called to tell his mother yesterday evening, somewhere round seven o'clock. He was over the moon about having a son. He'd been at the maternity home all day, and though he wasn't on speaking terms with most of the family he couldn't resist telling them the news.'

'Why wasn't he speaking to them?'

'He moved out when he decided to go straight, and went to live with his old Granny in Duck End. She's dead now, died last winter. And he didn't make himself popular with the family by marrying a Londoner—Bedingfields always marry Fairweathers or Catchpoles or Jermys. But his mother was pleased about the baby, and she gave him a cup of tea. He left about seven-thirty. He said he was going to meet somebody, but he didn't tell her who or where.'

'Where did he and his wife live?'

'They rented one of the houses on the new estate. It's about seven minutes' walk from the factory where his body was found. And that was where he used to work. Breckham Plastics, the firm was called. He was made redundant when the firm folded, and he's been unemployed ever since.'

'Short of money, then. And with a baby due... I know you said he was going straight, but a quiet meeting-place like that suggests that he was up to no good. Go and talk to his mates, Ian. I'll have a word with his wife as soon as she's recovered from the birth. WPC Hopkins has been to tell her parents, and they'll be fetching her from the maternity home and keeping her with them for the time being.'

'I expect she'll be discharged tonight,' said Wigby. 'My wife was sent out with our youngest within twenty-four hours. They run that maternity home like a production line, one in and two out, as fast as they can go.'

'Well, we'll find out as much as possible before we bother the girl with questions. I think we'll try the full weight of publicity on this one. Get Kevin Bedingfield's wedding photograph from his mother-in-law, and we'll do a press release for the front page of tomorrow's local paper, with an appeal for information from anyone who saw him after seven-thirty last night. And we'll emphasize the baby. That'll stir up public sympathy, and it should bring out people who might otherwise be reluctant to talk to us.'

Wigby swallowed his last mouthful of canteen sausage-roll and made for the door, but the internal telephone rang and Quantrill beckoned him back. A radio message had come in from Inspector Colman at the old Breckham Plastics factory. His search team had discovered a single bi-focal spectacle lens, lying near the place where Kevin Bedingfield had scuffled with his assailant.

'We've as good as got him, then,' Quantrill told Wigby with satisfaction. 'There's not much chance of two people wearing bi-focals with exactly the same prescription. John Colman is having the prescription analysed, and then you can start the leg-work, visiting all the opticians in the area and asking them to check their records. If we draw a blank there, we'll put an official notice in the opticians' journal. It may take a bit of time, but we'll get him for sure. And meanwhile, we've learned something else about him. We know he's tall and medium to thin; now we know that he wears glasses, and because they're bi-focals he's almost certainly over forty-five.'

'Doesn't sound much like any of Kevin Bedingfield's mates,' said Wigby. 'Doesn't sound like anybody who'd want to knock him down.'

# Chapter 24

The following morning at ten-thirty a tall thin man, wearing single lens horn-rimmed glasses and carrying a briefcase and a copy of the *East Anglian Daily Press,* walked into Breckham Market divisional police head-quarters and asked to see the officer in charge of the Kevin Bedingfield enquiry.

Quantrill knew instantly, when DC Wigby brought the man into his office, that he had seen him somewhere before. He looked about fifty, well-tailored and well-brushed; a professional man, but a worried one.

'Could I have your name, sir?'

'Reynolds, Alec Reynolds.' The man's grip on his newspaper tightened, but he spoke evenly and precisely. 'I have to tell you that I am the person you are looking for in connection with the death of the young man whose photograph is in this morning's paper. I met him by arrangement on Sunday evening, we had an argument, and I lost my temper. I struck him. It was a stupid act, which I can explain but not excuse by saying that I'd been drinking. He fell back heavily. I thought he was con-cussed, and I'm afraid I hurried off without checking whether he was injured. I was appalled to read this morn-ing of the consequences of my act, and I've come to give myself up.'

Wigby, sitting near the door behind Reynolds, gave a triumphant thumbs-up sign. The Chief Inspector was more circumspect: 'I see, sir.'

Quantrill leaned back in his chair and looked at the man with thoughtful affability. 'Tell me, are those the glasses you usually wear?'

Reynolds blinked. 'No. No, they're an old pair. Mine are broken.'

'Bi-focals?'

Reynolds gave him a startled, respectful look. 'As a matter of fact, they are.' He produced a pair of gold-rimmed spectacles from his briefcase. One bi-focal lens was missing. 'I had a slight scuffle with the young man, during which he knocked off my glasses. I think that was what made me lose my temper and hit him so hard. I had difficulty in finding them after he fell, and I was so anxious to get away that I didn't realize they were broken until I reached my car. Fortunately I keep this old pair in the car, so I was able to drive home.'

'We've already found the lens,' said Quantrill. 'We were about to start tracing you through the prescription, so you've saved us some work.'

Reynolds grimaced, evidently relieved that he had had the courage to give himself up. He looked round the Chief Inspector's untidy, functional office, as though by doing so he could familiarize himself with custodial surroundings. 'I expect you want me to make a statement?'

'Plenty of time for that, Mr Reynolds. I'd like a chat first.'

Quantrill began by asking Reynolds's address and occupation. He had recognized him, seconds after his entry, as the man who had accompanied Gillian Ainger at Athol Garrity's funeral. He wondered whether there was some link between the two deaths, and he wanted to see whether Reynolds would try to conceal his connection with the Aingers.

'And what brought you from Yarchester to Breckham Market?'

But the man was astute. He'd seen the detectives at Garrity's funeral, and so he would know that they recognized him. 'I'm a friend of the Rector and his wife,' he said. 'I quite often come over to see them on Sunday afternoons, and stay for Evensong as a matter of courtesy.'

'Ah, yes. But Kevin Bedingfield was no churchgoer, and I doubt he was a friend of the Aingers. How did you meet him?'

Reynolds hesitated. Then he admitted, 'I drink, and the Aingers don't. I usually call at the Coney and Thistle after I leave the Rectory. I happened to mention a week or two ago that I needed someone to do a few odd jobs, repairing the fence and digging the garden and so on, and one of the other customers said that he knew a young man who might be interested.'

DC Wigby, behind Reynolds, closed his eyes and blew out his cheeks and shook his head to indicate that Kevin Bedingfield's least favourite or competent activities would have been fence-mending and gardening.

'I see,' said Quantrill. 'And did this man you met in the pub give you Kevin's name?'

'No. He took my telephone number, and the young man rang me to arrange a meeting last Sunday.'

'Behind the old Breckham Plastics factory on the industrial estate?'

'Yes.'

Quantrill looked at him. Reynolds's expression remained composed, but a tic developed in his right cheek. Presently he added, 'It made sense. If he was drawing unemployment benefit and didn't intend to declare what he earned from me, he'd want to keep our meeting secret.'

'And you were prepared to condone the illegality?'

'I've come here to admit that I caused a man's death,' said Reynolds edgily. 'In the circumstances, it seems inappropriate for me to make moral judgements.'

His story leaked like a perished hosepipe, but Quantrill encouraged him to continue with it. 'So you met him as arranged. But then you had an argument with him—about what?'

Reynolds's tic persisted. 'About terms. He wanted more than I was prepared to pay.'

'And so you hit him? You, a civilized, well-educated man, a senior—'

The internal telephone rang. Quantrill snatched up the receiver: 'Yes?'

'Sorry to bother you, sir,' stammered the young probationary constable at the desk in the front office, jumping at the Chief Inspector's bark, 'but there's a gentleman to see you. He won't give his name, but he asked for you personally and he says it's important.'

'Ask him to wait. I'm busy.' Quantrill thumped the receiver down. 'Are you really trying to tell me,' he continued, glaring at Reynolds, 'that you were so incensed by a dispute over the price a man wanted for doing some odd jobs that you hit him so hard that you killed him?'

For the first time, the blood rose in Reynolds's cheeks. 'I didn't *mean* to kill him! For God's sake, you must realize that. I'm horrified by what's happened. That's why I had to come here and tell you.'

'Then let's have the whole truth while we're at it, Mr Reynolds. Because when Kevin Bedingfield's body was searched, a blank envelope containing a hundred pounds was found in one of his pockets. So I don't believe your story about the man in the pub and the odd jobs. I think that when Kevin contacted you, you agreed to meet him in that deserted place because you were making some kind of payoff. I think he was blackmailing you, and I want to know why.'

But Reynolds had regained his composure. 'I've told you as much as I intend to tell you,' he said. 'I'm prepared to make a statement on the lines of what I said when I first came into this office, but that's all.'

Quantrill's jaw tightened. 'Do you know what I think? I suspect that this crime you admit to, this unlawful killing, has some connection with the death of Athol Garrity, whose funeral we both attended some weeks ago. Has it?'

Reynolds said nothing.

Quantrill eased himself back into his chair and lit a small cigar. 'Let me tell you why I think this,' he said conversationally. 'Blackmail is a crime, and a nasty one. A blackmailer usually has a cruel—sometimes downright evil—streak in his or her makeup. Now, I never had occasion to meet young Kevin Bedingfield, but Detective Constable Wigby knew him quite well. Tell Mr Reynolds about Kevin, Wigby.'

Ian Wigby moved forward and gave the man an engaging smile. 'A nice young feller, Kevin,' he said. 'Not your sort, of course, Mr Reynolds—but then, he didn't have your advantages.'

Quantrill watched Reynolds impassively as the detective constable acknowledged Kevin Bedingfield's failings, and praised his attempts to break away from his family's influence and go straight. 'So you see, he wasn't the sneaky vicious type who spies and preys on people's weaknesses. But he was short of money, there's no doubt about that. Times are hard, Mr Reynolds, for people who aren't in safe civil-service jobs. So I reckon it's possible that if he got wind of something really criminal that somebody was trying to hide, he just might have been tempted to make a few quid out of it. Especially with the baby on the way.'

The muscle in Reynolds's cheek jumped again.

'Was that what happened?' asked Quantrill. 'Was Kevin trying to blackmail you because he had connected you with Athol Garrity's death last summer?'

Reynolds said nothing.

Quantrill slapped the flat of his hand on his desk. 'I want an answer. You've already admitted one involuntary killing. You've told us that you drink, you've told us that you can lose your temper, you've told us that in those circumstances you can hit out, and hit hard. Did you, last summer, for whatever reason, strike Athol Garrity and voluntarily or involuntarily cause his death?'

'No.' Reynolds sat very straight in his chair, his eyes behind his horn-rimmed glasses burning with indignation. 'No I did not strike Athol Garrity. No I did not in any way cause or contribute to his death. I have confessed to what I did on Sunday, and there is nothing else on my conscience.'

It was Quantrill's turn to sit silent. 'Then who was responsible for Garrity's death?' he pleaded at last.

Reynolds closed his briefcase and became briskly businesslike. 'I'd like to make a short statement as soon as possible about the events on Sunday evening. Apart from that, I intend to say nothing. And now I propose to exercise my right of telephoning my solicitor. I shall tell him exactly what I've told you, but I want him because I believe that he can arrange for me to be bailed. I'll accept whatever punishment the courts eventually decide—' he closed his eyes and swallowed hard, contemplating publicity, disgrace, imprisonment, '—but I'd prefer not to see the inside of a cell before I have to.'

Kevin Bedingfield's parents-in-law lived in a council maisonette in Pine Tree Walk, one of the network of new residential roads that spread bricks and cement over the fields that had once surrounded the old town. When Quantrill, accompanied by WPC Patsy Hopkins, called at number 237, he was turned away by a trim, pink-haired forty-year-old dragon with a voice so vigorously Cockney that he thought for a moment that she was Australian.

'No, you can't see Carole, she's feeding the baby. But you know what? Some cow from the Council forced her way in five minutes ago to see them. Health visitor, she says. You know what she's come for? To see whether this is a fit and proper place for my daughter to bring her baby! Bloody nerve... I'll give her "post-natal domestic environment"...'

Quantrill retreated. He was about to get into his car when a woman he knew approached on a bicycle. She was, he thought, younger than the new grandmother he had just met, but her face was so lined and her eyes so darkened with worry that she might have been fifteen years older.

He watched her dismount, prop her bicycle against a lamp-post and, wisely, padlock its wheels. Leaving WPC Hopkins in his car, he walked towards the woman and said, 'Good morning, Mrs Ainger.'

She started. For a moment her whole body drooped. Then she pulled herself together and gave him a nod, but said nothing.

'There's a health visitor at the Dents',' he said, as she

started to walk up the steps to their front door. 'I've just been turned away.'

She bit her lower lip uncertainly. 'Oh... I'll call back later, then, after I've been to the Over Sixties' Day Centre. My husband's gone to Yarchester, and when I saw the dreadful news in the paper I felt I had to see if there's anything I can do to help. The Bedingfields aren't churchgoers, but they're still our parishioners.'

Did she know about her friend Reynolds's confession, Quantrill wondered? Did she know about his involvement? 'If you'd like to wait, Mrs Ainger,' he suggested, 'you could sit in my car.'

She gave him a small, wry smile. 'No thank you, Mr Quantrill.'

'I wanted to ask about your father,' he said with peripheral truth. 'How is he? Still as difficult?'

'Not quite so bad, thank you.' She unlocked her bicycle again. 'He's easier to deal with in the summer, when he can get out into the garden. It was being cooped up in the house because of the snow that made him so obstreperous.'

'He doesn't go to the Boot, though?'

'No. He's quite at liberty to go if he wants to, he knows that. He's physically capable of getting there. But he seems to prefer pottering about in the garden.'

'Tell him I enquired after him,' said Quantrill. 'I'll drop in for a chat with him one day—later this week, perhaps.'

She had been about to ride off, but she paused with her left foot on the pedal and looked defiantly at the Chief Inspector.

'I hope you will do nothing of the kind. Oh, I'm sure my father would be pleased. He liked you. He thought he'd found a friend. He spoke of you as "Doug". But he's eighty-three years old, and easily confused, and I don't for a moment think that he realized you're a detective. And, frankly, I find your tactic of plying an old man with whisky in order to question him about our private lives entirely despicable. Good morning.'

It was not until she had cycled half-way down the road that Quantrill collected himself sufficiently to shut his sagging jaw.

# Chapter 25

He was in no mood, when he returned to the station to lunch off a canteen sandwich in his office, to be bounced upon outside the CID room by DC Wigby, with a doughnut partly in his hand and partly in his mouth, and to be asked, 'Guess who's just been to see me?'

'How the hell should I know?' snapped Quantrill. 'If you've anything to report, do it properly.'

'Sir,' acknowledged Wigby, gulping his mouthful and ostentatiously dropping the remainder of his doughnut into a waste-paper bin. But he was too ebullient to stay quashed. 'It was Mrs Muttock—you know, the grandmother of one of the boys who found Athol Garrity's body in Parson's Close. You'd told her to contact me if she heard the boys saying anything about the place. Seems they saw the photograph of Kevin Bedingfield on the front page of today's paper, and recognized him as a man who'd frightened them away from Parson's Close last summer.'

'Did they?' Quantrill beckoned the detective constable into his office. 'All right, I'm interested. Tell me more.'

'Well—sir—Mrs Muttock questioned the boys and it seems that they took it into their heads to go and play in Parson's Close one fine evening last summer. They saw the tent, and snooped round. It was closed up, but they found a pocket knife in the grass just outside, so they nicked it. That made them feel guilty. They ran away, through the long grass, and almost fell over a man and a girl. They assumed the man was the owner of the tent, and of the knife, but now they know it was Kevin Bedingfield.'

'We've no need to wonder what he and the girl were doing, I suppose.'

'Hard at it,' agreed Wigby; 'though you've got to allow for a bit of embroidery on Mrs Muttock's part. She hasn't had so much excitement since the skeleton was found. Anyway, Kevin was furious about the interruption, and he swore at the boys and told them he'd give them a thrashing if he ever caught them in Parson's Close again. And that's all Mrs Muttock had to tell me, except that she insisted on handing the pocket knife in. But—'

Quantrill was already making his own deductions, but it seemed unjust to take them out of Wigby's mouth, and so he merely looked encouraging.

'—what I think it means is that Kevin and the girl used Parson's Close regularly last summer when they wanted a bit of love-making. Kevin was living at the time with his Granny, just on the other side of the allotments from Parson's Close, and Carole lived on the new estate, across the by-pass, so it'd make an ideal meeting-place. They might well have seen or heard something going on while they were hidden in the long grass—something connected with Athol Garrity.'

'That's it,' said Quantrill. 'That's just the connection we needed. Get yourself another doughnut, to celebrate. I'm going back to Pine Tree Walk to find out what I can from Carole Bedingfield.'

He didn't relish the thought of having to revive, with a newly widowed girl, the memories of her pre-marital lovemaking. But her pink-haired mother assured him, in answer to his doorstep enquiry, that her daughter was quite calm.

'Well, it's having the baby. It takes you that way for the first day or two. She's in another world. She knows about Kevin, of course, but she hasn't really grasped it yet. It's as if he's out at the pub—well, that's where he generally was. I wouldn't have minded so much if he'd gone to a nice place like the Concorde, where he could have taken Carole, but he would keep going back to that dirty old Boot in the town. Me and her Dad were against her marrying into local riffraff, but she wouldn't listen. Not that we'd have wished him dead, mind. Carole was properly in love with him, and I dread to think what sort of state she'll be in when she realizes she'll never see him again.'

She took her visitors across a tiny, spotless hall and into an overheated living room. Carole Bedingfield, a plump and healthy eighteen, sat on a settee with her feet up, evidently luxuriating in her mother's care. She wore a pretty dressing gown and fluffy slippers, and she exuded milky warmth and pride and contentment. There was a vague soft smile on her face, and her ringed left hand was stretched out to rock the elaborately frilled reproduction of a Victorian bassinet that stood by her side.

Patsy Hopkins, tall, elegant, no baby-lover but an experienced policewoman, firmly diverted Mrs Dent's attention from the interview by admiring her sleeping grandson. Quantrill began to put his questions to Carole

Bedingfield as delicately as he knew how, and she answered him with composure. Her voice was quieter than her mother's, though sharper than any native Suffolk girl's.

No, she'd had no idea where Kevin was going after he left the maternity home on Sunday night; to the Boot to celebrate, she supposed.

Yes, Kevin was worried sick about money when Breckham Plastics closed down. But for the past week or two he'd seemed happier about his prospects. He'd said he thought there might be something in the pipeline, though he didn't tell her what. When he was with her at the maternity home, just before the baby came, he had said she wasn't to worry about money because he'd definitely got something lined up.

She agreed that she knew Parson's Close, the field behind the street where Kevin's Granny lived. That was where they used to go last summer, she added, with a happily reminiscent smile. They saw a tent, up at the top of the field, and once or twice they saw a man near it, but they didn't bother him and he didn't bother them. ''Spect he never even saw us,' she said, giggling softly.

'But did *you* see or hear anything—anything at all unusual—while you were in Parson's Close?'

Blushing, she told him about the untimely interruption from the children. Quantrill persisted, and eventually she remembered something else.

'It was after dark, but moonlight, a lovely warm evening—the day after my birthday. I was eighteen on 28 July. Kevin and I were, well—you know—and we could hear something moving slowly down towards us from the top of the field. I was afraid it might be a bull but Kevin— he was on top so he could see what was happening—said it was a feller carrying something big and heavy on his

back. Then Kevin said he'd fallen over, and we could hear
him swearing. We were giggling like anything, and hoping
he couldn't hear us. Then he got up, groaning and moaning, and started dragging whatever it was that he'd been
carrying. He lugged it down as far as the road, and then
we lost interest.'

'Was it the man you'd seen near the tent?'

'Oh no, he was young. This one was old. Kevin had an
idea that he was an old man he'd seen once or twice in the
Boot.'

'And he was moaning and groaning, you said. Did you
hear any words?'

'Well, you know: "Oh, me back," and things like that.
And something about bloody ozzies...'

A small mew, no stronger than a kitten's, began to
emanate from the bassinet. Quantrill thanked the girl and
moved into the hall. WPC Hopkins and Mrs Dent followed.

'What I don't understand,' the policewoman said, as
Mrs Dent opened the front door for them, 'is why your
daughter didn't report to us what she'd seen and heard in
Parson's Close. We put out a public appeal only a few
weeks ago, asking for just this kind of information.'

Mrs Dent stared at her blankly. 'I never knew anything about that. I don't suppose Carole did either.'

'It was on the front page of the local paper.'

Trim and urban, Mrs Dent looked out from her
maisonette doorway at the rows of low-cost housing and
the parade of shops that formed one section of Breckham
Market new town. It was characterless, anonymous. Its
inhabitants might have been living in any part of England.

'What would we want with the local paper?' she
asked. 'It's about nothing but Suffolk.'

The police officers walked down the concrete steps,

just as a wail of panic and desolation arose from inside
the house. Carole Bedingfield, left alone for the first time,
had begun to sense the enormity of her loss.

'Mum! Oh, Mum...oh Kevin...'

'So now we know how Athol Garrity's body came to
be in the bushes at the bottom of Parson's Close,' said
Patsy Hopkins as they drove away.

'Yes—and that's all we do know,' agreed Quantrill,
grateful for the company of a junior colleague who didn't
jump eagerly to conclusions. 'We don't know why
Reynolds was being blackmailed by Kevin Bedingfield,
and we still don't know how Athol Garrity died.'

# Chapter 26

As Quantrill walked through the front office, the prematurely grey station sergeant called to him.

'Message for you, sir. Mrs Ainger, the Rector's wife, rang ten minutes ago to say that her father is missing. She last saw him when she went out, about ten-thirty this morning. She returned just before one, but she spent some time searching the house and gardens before contacting us. I've sent a patrol car to tour the town. The old gentleman's over eighty, and—'

'I know him, Larry.' With a sense of foreboding Quantrill added, 'Someone called to see me this morning, when I was busy. Just after eleven, I think. "A gentleman", so PC Phipps said. Did you see him?'

'No, sir. He must have come in while I was in the charge room. I'll get hold of young Phipps for you.'

Young Phipps was summoned from the cells, where he was listening saucer-eyed to an older constable's hyperbolical account of what-you-want-to-look-out-for-when-dealing-with-some-of-the-villains-we-get-in-here. He was a lanky nineteen, desperately worried that he would not survive his probationary year.

Quantrill described old Henry Bowers.

'That was him, sir,' agreed Phipps nervously, 'but he wouldn't give me his name. He said it was a personal matter. He didn't seem to know your rank, and I wasn't sure at first who he meant. He just said "Doug".'

'Why on earth didn't you tell me he was old?' Quantrill demanded. 'If I'd known that—'

PC Phipps reddened. 'Sir, I couldn't say so in front of him. It wouldn't have been polite.'

'Didn't you ask him to wait?'

'Yes, sir. He sat down on the bench for a few minutes, but he was very fidgety. Then he said he couldn't wait any longer, but he'd like to leave a message for you.' The young constable took out his pocket book. 'He didn't tell me that the message was urgent, sir,' he pointed out defensively. 'He just said it was something he thought you'd want to know. *Tell Doug,*' he read out, puzzled, '*that it wasn't too much beer. I used a cushion.*'

'Oh my God—' said Quantrill. 'No, don't worry, Phipps, it's not your fault.' He turned to Sergeant Lamb. 'Never mind about searching the streets. Try the trees at the top of Parson's Close. Try the spinney by the recreation ground. Try the Mere. Try the river.'

'I'm sorry, Mrs Ainger.'

She stood with her back to him, staring out of the Rectory drawing-room window. 'Where was he found?' she asked.

'In the river, just below Castle Meadow. I'm afraid I'll have to ask you to make a formal identification.'

'Can I leave it until my husband gets back from Yarchester?'

'Yes, of course.'

She faced him, her head high. 'My father was depressed by his increasing infirmity,' she said. 'He loved gardening, but he hurt his back last year and since then—'

Quantrill shook his head. 'There's no need to cover for him anymore, Mrs Ainger. This is a private conversation, so let's be frank. I know how your father hurt his back, and I know why he took his own life. He came to tell me this morning.'

She sat down suddenly and began to weep, her tears a compound of grief, shock, and relief that the weeks of concealment were over. He walked to the window and looked out at the neglected April garden while he waited for her to compose herself.

Presently she said, 'Did he tell you how he killed Athol?'

'I'm not entirely clear about the details, but I think he smothered Garrity with a cushion while the man was in a drunken sleep.'

'A cushion? Oh yes—one went missing from this room last summer. I had too much on my mind to bother about it, but I found it a few weeks ago in the toolshed.'

'When did you discover that your father had killed Garrity?'

'We never knew for sure. We guessed, that's all.'

'And I wondered about him, but I couldn't see his motive.' Quantrill sat down opposite her. 'Please tell me what it was, Mrs Ainger. You've no need to protect him now.'

She hesitated. 'So much of it concerns our private life, Robin's and mine.'

'Policemen have personal problems too. I know a married chief inspector who once fell disastrously in love with another woman...'

Gillian Ainger gave him a damp smile of acknowledgement and began, haltingly, to tell him what he needed to know. She omitted to spell out the nature of her husband's relationship with Janey Rolph; whether she was defending him or salving her own pride, Quantrill wasn't sure, but he didn't pursue the point. It was obvious that passions had been aroused more strongly than she was prepared to admit.

'And what happened after Janey Rolph finally drove away?'

'The four of us—Robin and I, Dad and Alec Reynolds—came back into the house. Alec had been drinking too much to drive home—he had troubles of his own, poor man—so we offered him a bed. After he'd gone upstairs Robin and I sat in the kitchen for a long time, talking. We thought Dad was in here watching television, but when I started to lock the house he came in from outside. It was a warm, moonlit night, and he said he'd been walking round the garden. I didn't realize until the next day that he'd hurt his back, but I had no reason not to believe that he'd ricked it while he was digging. I suppose he had trouble moving Athol's body?'

'That was how he did the damage. But you didn't suspect at the time that he'd killed Garrity?'

'Why should we? We had no idea the man was dead. We went to bed sick with fear, convinced that our story would be all round the town the next day. But everything was normal, and when I took a look in Parson's Close and saw that Athol's tent had gone, we assumed that he had moved on. It didn't surprise me, on reflection, because he wasn't in any way an unkind or malicious man. Poor Athol...we were so relieved that we simply tried to forget that he'd ever existed.'

'So it was the finding of the skeleton that first made you suspect your father?'

'We could see that it was a dreadful possibility. And

then, when you started asking questions about Athol's tent, Robin and I searched our outbuildings and found it hidden under some sacking in the toolshed, with the drawing-room cushion. Dad was the only one who ever went to that shed. We still didn't know for sure, of course, but I couldn't possibly ask him; what would I have done if he'd said "Yes"? I couldn't turn in my own father. And Robin wouldn't, because if he'd done so the whole story would have emerged.'

'And where does Alec Reynolds come into this?'

She bit her lower lip in dismay. 'Oh, poor Alec—the shock of Dad's death made me completely forget what he's been going through. He came here early this morning, after the news of Kevin Bedingfield's death appeared in the local paper, and told me what had happened on Sunday night. He said that he was going to admit responsibility, but that he wouldn't involve us in any way. I think that Dad probably overheard, and decided to make his own confession...oh God, what a tragedy it's been.'

Quantrill waited patiently while she wept again. Then he said, 'But I still don't understand why Alec Reynolds was being blackmailed.'

'He wasn't, that's part of the tragedy. Kevin Bedingfield came to see me—I didn't know his name at the time—when the newspaper publicity about Athol was at its height. He suggested, in quite a friendly way, that he thought my father knew something about it. He also told me that he was unemployed, and that his wife was pregnant, and I gave him some money without being asked. Just five pounds at first.'

'And then he started to make a habit of coming?'

'Yes, every week or ten days. It wasn't at all alarming. He'd call for a chat, and show me his wedding photographs, but then he'd tell me how expensive everything was, and how difficult he found it to manage with the baby on the way, and I'd give him some more. He never once threatened me.'

'Did you tell your husband?'

'I couldn't. Robin had been through so much. He had some kind of breakdown after Janey left, and then when he realized that you suspected him of murder he nearly cracked up completely. No, Kevin was my problem, not Robin's. But I had to confide in someone, so I told Alec Reynolds. He pointed out that I was being blackmailed, and volunteered to frighten Kevin off.'

'You knew the boy's name by that time?'

'He wouldn't give me his surname, or his address. I didn't want him to keep coming here, in case Robin suspected anything, so I asked him to suggest a meeting-place on the other side of the by-pass, where I wouldn't be recognized. Alec went instead of me. I gave him some money to take as a final gift for Kevin's family.'

'It was found on his body. A hundred pounds?'

'Yes, the last of my savings. Not that he'd asked for it. I sent it as conscience-money, I suppose. Dad had committed a dreadful crime with the intention of protecting me, and I was trying to assuage some of my guilt.'

She fell silent. Then she said, 'Dad really took to you, Mr Quantrill. And I did you an injustice when I spoke to you this morning, simply because I wanted to keep you away from him. He knew quite well that you were a policeman—his only confusion was about your rank. He'd have been tremendously pleased if you'd called to chat to him, in these last few weeks. I think he wanted to tell you about Athol's death, and was trying to find a way of doing so without involving me.'

'I felt sure that he could tell me something. But I didn't talk to him solely for that reason, Mrs Ainger. I liked him, and I liked the way he spoke of you. He told me that he thought the world of you, and that he'd do anything for you.'

'And so he did, poor foolish old man...' A large tear slid down one of her cheeks, and she wiped it away with her fingers. 'What happens now?'

'There'll be an inquest into his death, of course. But he didn't give his name when he called to see me at the station this morning, so the only thing we have on record is your telephone call to say that he was missing.'

'Thank you. But what are you going to do about Athol's death?'

'Nothing. That inquest has already been held, and the file has been closed. It would serve no useful purpose to have the verdict amended. I'll simply put a note on the file, for the record.'

She blew her nose. 'I'm indebted to you, Mr Quantrill.'

'Don't be. In fact, I didn't see your father this morning. He asked for me, but I said I was too busy, so he left me a message and went. If I'm not carrying out my duty to the letter now, it's by way of apology to him.'

Quantrill got up to go. 'What you and your husband need now is a holiday,' he said.

'Probably. But we'll soon be leaving Breckham Market for good. Even if none of this is made public, we've broken too many trusts to stay here. That's why Robin is in Yarchester today, arranging for us to move to one of the livings in the city. It's a poor parish, and the stipend is a good deal less than we're getting here, but at least we'll feel rather more anonymous. It's a step down for Robin, but he's given up the hopes he once had of high office.'

'You'll be missed in Breckham,' said Quantrill,

knowing it to be true. 'You've both been thought of very highly.'

Colour flooded her cheeks. 'That's just the point, isn't it? We've been expected to live exemplary lives, and we seem to have succeeded in giving that impression. But look at the cost of our deception: Athol Garrity dead; Michael Dade dead; Kevin Bedingfield dead, his wife widowed at eighteen, his new-born baby fatherless; Alec Reynolds's good name and career ruined; my father dead. And I blame myself, Mr Quantrill. None of this would have happened if I hadn't insisted on making friends outside the parish.'

'We can't assume responsibility for other people's actions,' he told her briskly, 'and no one could possibly blame you for wanting to extend your social circle. As I see it—' he thought of Martin Tait's description of the stunningly red-haired girl who had played the major part in the destructive process, '—your mistake was simply to have been so unguarded in your choice of friends.'

# Part 4—New Hampshire, Last Fall

# Chapter 27

At Coburg College, a small private university set high in the hills of New Hampshire, the President was holding a reception for the Faculty, which on this occasion was extended to include graduate assistants.

One of the new Faculty wives, whose husband had been appointed Professor of European History, sipped her glass of white wine and looked about her shyly. Mary-Jo Daubeny Brown was what the Edwardians would have recognized as a fine figure of a woman: five feet ten inches tall, almost exactly the same height as her husband, but more generous in both proportion and disposition. Among the crowds at Ohio State she had felt relatively inconspicuous, but here, in the rarefied air of Coburg, she had become self-conscious.

Other Faculty wives were either elegantly East Coast or alarmingly intellectual. Some were both. Mary-Jo Daubeny Brown, who felt that she had neither grace nor intellect, and who had no children to talk about, wondered on what level she could ever establish a relationship with any of them. She was almost afraid to open her mouth. It was only last week that her husband, forty years old and a specialist in eighteenth-century political theory, had made a peevish Bostonian pronouncement about the Louisiana accent that had so charmed him in their early years together. She was, he said, the only woman he knew who needed three syllables to pronounce the word 'red'.

As she stood on the fringe of an animated conversation, smiling and nodding and juggling with wine glass and canapé, Mary-Jo's purse slipped from beneath her arm. It was caught as it fell by a delicate girl with a brilliant flame of hair who said, when thanked, 'No trouble. Being as wretchedly short as I am has to have *some* advantages.'

Mary-Jo warmed to her instantly. The girl wasn't American, and, despite the fact that she was being eyed with covert interest by most of the male members of the Faculty, she looked wistfully friendless.

'You must be English?' said Mary-Jo, thinking that she recognized Michael Caine's film Cockney.

'No, Australian. I'm a new graduate assistant in the Department of English. But I've just spent two years in England, taking my M. Phil.'

They exchanged names. 'Have you been back home, between universities?' asked Mary-Jo.

'No, I came straight on here. I spent August in New York and Washington, sightseeing, and I nearly turned into a grease spot. The heat was so sticky and oppressive, and I longed for the beaches at home.'

The girl paused, evidently overwhelmed by a wave of homesickness. Then she brightened. 'But Coburg is magnificent. I've always longed to see New England in the Fall. Most of the trees in Australia are evergreen, you see; we have nothing like this. Autumn in England is quite pretty, but the colours here are beyond anything I could ever imagine.'

'Oh, for me too,' said Mary-Jo quickly. 'I'm a stranger here myself. They tell me there's a fine scenic route through the hills, but I don't care to drive it alone. Now, if you'd like to come along—?'

'Are you sure I wouldn't be intruding?'

'I'd be glad of your company. We—that's my husband Francis, the one with the brown moustache—have just moved into one of the Faculty houses on the other side of the campus. It was built for a family of ten, I guess— we're only two, and we're feeling a little lost in it. So if you'd care to drop by for a cup of coffee, or a meal, I'd be very happy to see you.'

The girl's face brightened. 'Do you really mean it? That would be wonderful. I've been in the States for three months, but I've never yet been inside a private house.'

'Well, then, of course you must come!' Pleased and purposeful, Mary-Jo scribbled down her address and telephone number. 'Now you come over any time, Janey,' she said warmly. 'Any time at all...'